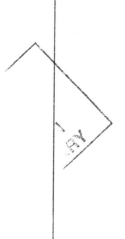

LUCY DANIELS

Dalmatian
– in the –
Dales

Illustrations by Ann Baum

Hodder
Children's
Books

a division of Hodder Headline Limited

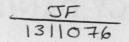

Special thanks to Sue Bentley

**Thanks also to C. J. Hall, B.Vet.Med., M.R.C.V.S., for reviewing
the veterinary information contained in this book.**

Animal Ark is a trademark of Working Partners Limited
Text copyright © 2002 Working Partners Limited
Created by Working Partners Limited, London W6 0QT
Original series created by Ben M. Baglio
Illustrations copyright © 2002 Ann Baum

First published in Great Britain in 2002
by Hodder Children's Books

For more information about Animal Ark,
please contact www.animalark.co.uk

10 9 8 7 6 5 4 3 2 1

A Catalogue record for this book is available from
the British Library

ISBN 0 340 85114 7

Typeset by Avon Dataset Ltd, Bidford-on-Avon, Warks

Printed and bound in Great Britain by
Clays Ltd, St Ives plc

Hodder Children's Books
a division of Hodder Headline Limited
338 Euston Road
London NW1 3BH

One

'Look over there!' Mandy Hope called to her best friend, James Hunter. She pointed across the moor to the edge of the woods.

'Hang on a minute! I've just got to get this shot.' James crouched down and pointed his camera at some rabbits in the distance, playing chase on the wind-blown slopes. 'Oh, they've all dived into their burrows.'

'Never mind! I've just seen something even better.' Mandy was hardly able to contain her excitement. 'Fallow deer!'

'Oh, wow! That's great!' James jumped up and pushed his glasses on to the bridge of his nose.

'Let's go!' Mandy set off up the hill, white limestone pebbles crunching beneath her boots. The sky was a clear brilliant blue over the rolling hills. Drystone walls snaked across acres of open space.

Normally, when she wasn't at school, Mandy helped out in her parents' veterinary surgery in Welford, but today was Saturday, and the surgery closed at lunchtime. Mandy and James had come to the moor to take photographs for the *Woodland Wildlife* magazine's competition.

'Those trees are the start of Glisterdale Forest,' Mandy said, as James fell into step with her. 'Honey-Mum and Sprite live there. I'd really love to see the two of them again.'

'Me too,' James agreed.

Honey-Mum was a fallow deer who had adopted the orphaned fawn.

'I bet Sprite has grown a lot by now,' Mandy said, thinking of the gentle fawn with her reddish-gold coat and light spots. She felt a pang as she remembered finding the tiny newborn bundle, helpless and alone behind the Old School House in Welford.

'She's been running free with the herd for months now,' said James. 'I wonder if we'll still recognise her?'

'I'd know her anywhere!' Mandy was confident. 'Besides, wasn't Sprite fitted with a blue ear tag?'

James grinned. 'Oh, yes. Well, that should help.'

Just inside the woods, they paused beneath a massive oak which was laden with fat green acorns. Mandy looked around, but could see no sign of the deer.

'They must have gone into the forest,' said James. He was probably right. But Mandy couldn't help feeling disappointed. She'd really been hoping to see Sprite and Honey-Mum again. Just then she noticed a narrow, flattened path that led through the bracken.

'Look – a deer trail. Come on, let's follow it!' Mandy started to push her way through the dry rust-coloured bracken.

James paused to fiddle with his camera. 'I'll put this on automatic focus. Then as soon as we catch sight of any deer, I'm ready for action.'

'OK,' Mandy said. James was brilliant with technical equipment. He knew all about light meters and lenses. They moved quietly down the trail. It led them into a grassy glade, bordered on all sides by trees. The spreading branches of one huge beech tree hung low enough to brush the grass.

'Lots of juicy shoots within reach. Just what deer like,' Mandy whispered. 'I reckon we might see some if we wait here.'

James nodded. 'This looks a good spot.' He crouched down to wait beside Mandy. All was quiet, except for the piping of a robin. A blackbird hopped into view and began foraging for grubs in the fallen leaves.

A few minutes passed, then Mandy stiffened. Stepping slowly into the autumn sunlight were five fallow deer. Mandy held her breath as she watched the group, three adult females and two fawns, make their way daintily across the grass. 'Aren't they beautiful!' she murmured. Her eyes flickered over the deers' rich, glossy chestnut coats. 'But I don't think any of those are Honey-Mum.'

'The light coming through the trees is perfect.' James was already raising his camera. 'Now – don't you move . . .'

Click. He pressed the button, just as the doe at the head of the group stopped and jerked her head round. She gave a sharp little bark, stamped her hoof and raised her tail to show the white fur underneath.

'She's warning them of danger,' Mandy said.

'Maybe they can smell us,' suggested James.

Mandy licked the tip of her finger and held it up. She shook her head. 'We're upwind of them. It's something else.'

'I don't see anything,' said James.

All at once the little herd took off. Leaping high over the grass, white tails bobbing, they headed for cover.

Suddenly there was a frantic rustling in the undergrowth to one side of them.

James spun round. 'What's that?'

'Oh!' Mandy's blue eyes widened as a large black and white dog came crashing through the bushes. 'It's a Dalmatian!'

The Dalmatian raced across the clearing. But it seemed to tire suddenly, and stopped, panting heavily. Mandy watched as it lifted up one front paw. She could see tremors moving over its black and white coat as its sides heaved. 'I think it's hurt its foot,' she said. She peered through the trees, expecting an owner with a lead to appear at any moment. But no one came.

'Maybe it's a stray?' suggested James.

Mandy shook her head doubtfully. 'A pedigree Dalmatian wouldn't be a stray. Besides, it looks too well-fed. And look – it's wearing a collar.'

'There might be a name and address on it,' said James.

'Good thinking,' Mandy replied. I'm going to see if I can make friends with it.'

She moved forward slowly. As she got closer she could see that the dog was a female. On one back leg, her spots formed an unusual shape just like a paw print. The Dalmatian's ears were laid flat against her head. Dipping her neck, she whined softly and licked her sore paw.

'Hello, girl,' Mandy said softly. 'Aren't you lovely?'

The dog didn't look up. Mandy frowned in concentration as she edged forward. Just a bit closer and she might be able to grab the collar. Slowly Mandy stretched out her hand.

The Dalmatian turned her head and seemed to see Mandy for the first time. She gave a violent start and jumped sideways. She looked ready to take off again at any moment.

'Don't be scared. I won't hurt you,' Mandy crooned. She made encouraging noises and rubbed her fingertips together.

The Dalmatian looked at her for a second with scared dark-brown eyes. Then she whined softly, turned tail and darted away through the trees.

James dashed after her. Mandy followed, but

she was only in time to see a black and white shape sprinting away into the distance. Soon it was no more than a speck between the trees.

'That dog really can run!' James puffed, stopping dead and resting his hands on his knees.

'You're not kidding!' Mandy's shoulders sagged. 'We hadn't a hope of catching her, even with a sore paw. Dad says Dalmatians can run all day without getting tired. They were bred to run beside carriages.'

'I wonder why that one seemed so exhausted then?' James mused.

Mandy frowned. 'That's a good point. Maybe she wasn't really tired, just lost and confused.'

'She was dead nervous. She nearly jumped out of her skin when she saw you,' James reminded her.

'I know. That was a bit strange too, wasn't it?' Mandy said. She was beginning to feel really worried about the dog. 'I hate to think of the poor thing out here all alone and injured.'

'Me too. I'd be worried sick if it was Blackie,' James said. Blackie was his boisterous young Labrador.

Mandy made up her mind. 'I think we should go after her and try to find her.'

'Me too. But where do we start?' asked James. 'We can't search the entire forest on foot. Besides, it will be starting to get dark soon.'

'That's true,' Mandy admitted. 'But we could search for a bit longer if we had some help. And a Land-rover . . .'

James caught on fast. 'Like your dad's?'

Mandy grinned. 'Exactly! I reckon he should have finished up at High Cross by now. He said he'd give us a lift home. Let's go and meet him.'

Mandy and James walked back along the road that curved around the edge of Glisterdale Forest. They had almost reached the stony track that led up to Lydia Fawcett's farm when the Animal Ark Land-rover appeared round a bend in front of them.

'Here's Dad!' Mandy raised her hand in a wave.

The Land-rover drew to a halt. 'Hi, you two,' said Adam Hope.

'Hi, Dad.' Mandy opened the door and jumped into the front seat.

James climbed into the back. 'Hello, Mr Hope.'

'How's Lydia? And Houdini?' Mandy asked. She always wanted to know all the details of her parents' visit to the local farms. Especially when it was to one of her friends.

'Lydia's fine. She said to say hello. One of her goats had broken a tooth,' her dad answered, grinning. 'And Houdini is his usual self, full of beans and getting into trouble.'

Mandy and James laughed. They knew all about Houdini. Lydia's favourite goat had been named after the famous escapologist.

'How did the wildlife photography go?' asked Adam Hope.

Mandy glanced over her shoulder at James. 'It kind of . . . didn't, did it James?'

'No. Not really,' admitted James.

Adam Hope checked his driver's mirror and edged the Land-rover away from the verge. 'Well, don't look so glum. There's still plenty of time to get your entries in.'

'We know. It's not that,' Mandy said, glancing at James. 'It's just that we were watching some deer when this Dalmatian came dashing through the woods. She seemed lost and we think she'd hurt her foot. So – if we're not in too much of a hurry to get back, I thought . . .'

'You want me to drive around the dales looking for it?' guessed her dad.

Mandy nodded. 'Can we?'

'Are you sure there wasn't an owner somewhere

in the woods?' Adam Hope asked. 'I know you, Mandy. Some animals just don't need rescuing!'

Mandy was almost certain that the dog had been alone, but she couldn't be sure. 'We didn't see anyone looking for their dog,' she said carefully.

'But the Dalmatian didn't look like a stray either,' James pointed out. 'It had a collar on.'

'Yes. Though I didn't get close enough to read any details,' Mandy rushed on. 'And I'm sure she had hurt her foot, Dad. Even though she ran off again . . .'

'Whoa! OK, you two! I'm convinced!' Adam Hope held his hands up and grinned at Mandy. 'You'd better show me where she was heading.'

'Thanks, Dad!' she breathed.

Mandy directed her dad to the edge of the woods where she and James had last seen the Dalmatian. Mr Hope drove up and down the road, but there was no sign of her.

'Maybe we should call into some of the car parks?' suggested James. 'Lots of dog-walkers use them.'

'Good idea,' Mandy said. 'I'll ask anyone if they've seen a Dalmatian.'

But even though they spoke to several ramblers who were just returning to their car, no one had seen a lone Dalmatian.

Half an hour later, Mr Hope pulled to a halt. 'There's a lot of space round here to cover,' he said. 'That dog could be anywhere by now.'

Mandy stared out at the winding road. Even she had to admit to feeling discouraged. The light over the dales was beginning to fade now. The sky had turned to violet and tiny lights glimmered from the hill farms on the steep slopes.

'I think it's time we went home,' Adam Hope said.

'OK.' Mandy admitted defeat. 'Thanks for looking, anyway, Dad.'

'Yes, thanks, Mr Hope,' said James.

'No problem.' Adam Hope switched on the headlights. 'There may have been an owner around, even if you and James didn't see one. I wouldn't be surprised if your Dalmatian isn't tucked up warm at home by now.'

'I hope so,' Mandy said, but she wasn't convinced. For some reason that she couldn't explain to herself, she felt sure that the Dalmatian was out there somewhere, hurt and frightened and probably hungry too. She stared gloomily ahead at the road as they sped down the valley.

Adam Hope began to sing. 'All things bright and beautiful . . .' His rich baritone voice filled the car.

Despite herself, Mandy smiled. Her dad was in the church choir and he had a habit of bursting into song at any time. She glanced at James in the mirror and rolled her eyes. Her dad could be so embarrassing.

But James just shrugged and grinned.

'. . . all things wise and wonderful . . .' Mr Hope continued the hymn. 'My tummy tells me it's almost supper time. Macaroni cheese tonight. With lots of toasted cheese on top.'

'Da-ad!' Mandy protested. 'What about your diet?'

'I'm on a new one now. It's called the seafood diet.' Her dad grinned, a glint in his eye.

Mandy groaned. 'I know. You see-food and you eat it, right? That's a terrible joke!'

Adam Hope pretended to look hurt. Mandy and James laughed.

The Land-rover's engine changed tone as they sped up out of the valley. Mandy began to think of the animals she was going to check on as soon as she got back to Animal Ark. Animals that were too sick to go home were kept in the residential unit overnight. At the moment there was a kitten with a broken leg and a rabbit which had had an operation to remove a tumour.

Just then, Mr Hope's mobile phone rang.

He pulled over to the side of the road before answering. 'Hello? Oh, Mr Western. What can I do for you?'

Sam Western's loud voice came out of the mobile. Mandy and James caught a few words of what he was saying.

'Just happened . . . get over here, man. Now!'

Mandy glanced over her shoulder at James. What was Sam Western up to? The tough local businessman owned the woods where they had just been. He had no love of wildlife and ran his farms strictly for profit.

'Try and calm down,' Mr Hope was saying into the mobile. 'Just tell me what happened.' His good-natured face became serious as he listened.

'Sounds bad,' James hissed to Mandy.

Adam Hope spoke calmly, his brow furrowed in concentration. 'OK. I understand. Now – tell me where you are. Good, I'm quite near to you. I'll be there in a few minutes.'

Mandy waited tensely for her dad to finish speaking. 'What's wrong, Dad?' she asked.

'We have to go straight back up to Glisterdale,' her dad replied, as he checked the road in his driving mirror. 'Hang on, you two.' He swung the Land-rover into a nearby gateway and turned round.

'What's going on?' Mandy asked, a cold feeling creeping over her.

'It's one of Sam Western's bulldogs, Boris,' Adam Hope explained. 'He's been shot.'

'What!' Mandy felt shocked. She completely forgot her dislike of the dog's owner, she was so upset for the dog. 'Poor Boris,' she gasped. Her mind whirled. Who would shoot a dog?

Two

'There's Sam Western's car by the lamppost!' Mandy leaned forward in her seat as her father drew into the car park. In the headlights, she caught sight of Sam Western kneeling on the ground. A bulky white shape was lying on a rug beside him. It was Boris. The bulldog's back legs were streaked with blood, and he wasn't moving.

'Oh no,' Mandy gasped.

As Adam Hope parked the Land-rover and got out, Sam Western stood up. His grey-blond hair stuck up in tufts where he'd run his hands through it.

'Thank goodness you're here!' said Mr Western.

Mr Hope went straight over to the injured dog and knelt down. 'Mandy, would you get my bag, please?' he called over his shoulder.

'OK, Dad.' Mandy hurried to fetch it from the back of the Land-rover. She dashed back with it and handed it to her dad. 'Here you are.'

'Thanks, love.' Adam Hope ran his expert hands over Boris. After a few moments, he looked up. 'These are gunshot wounds all right, Mr Western. There are pellets embedded in his back legs.'

Mandy felt her stomach lurch.

'What happened exactly?' Adam Hope asked.

Sam Western looked impatient. 'It's like I said. I let Boris off for a run in the woods. Then I came and sat in my Land-rover. I had a couple of calls to make. Next thing I know, Boris has come back and he's got blood on him. When I think back, I might have heard shots, but I was on the phone and I didn't take much notice. I thought it was probably one of the farmers shooting rabbits.'

'Did you have a look around for someone you might recognise?' Mr Hope asked.

Sam Western shook his head. 'I was too worried about Boris. The minute I saw what had happened, I phoned you.'

Adam Hope nodded sympathetically. 'That's

understandable. I think Boris has been very lucky. Some of these wounds are quite deep, but he should be all right. I'll need to take him back to the surgery to do X-rays before I remove the pellets.'

'Is that to check for any damage to the bone?' Mandy asked.

Her dad nodded. 'And I want to make sure that no major blood vessels have been ruptured.'

'Never mind all the questions.' Sam Western elbowed James aside. 'Can't you do something for him now? Look at him – he's trembling all over.'

'That's due to the shock.' Adam Hope got Mandy to pass him a bottle and a sterile packet, containing a syringe. I'm going to give him something for that right now.'

'Poor boy,' Mandy said soothingly to Boris. 'This will make you feel better.'

Boris lifted his big square head. Mandy saw that his dark eyes were clouded with pain. Lifting one of his wrinkled jowls, he gave a soft growl.

'Be careful, Mandy,' warned her dad.

'I know, Dad,' Mandy replied. She understood that animals could be unpredictable when they were in pain.

Sam Western frowned. 'Do we have to have these kids getting in the way?'

'It's OK, Mandy's used to helping in the surgery,'
said Adam Hope. 'And if they hadn't persuaded
me to stay up at the dales, I'd have taken a lot
longer to get to you and Boris.'

Sam Western ignored him. 'I'll hold Boris's
collar while you give him the injection.'

Mandy and James watched as Sam Western took
hold of Boris's steel-studded collar. 'It's all right,
boy,' he said gruffly, smoothing the dog's ear. Boris
gave a feeble bark and tried to lick his owner's hand.

Mr Hope injected Boris in the loose skin at his neck. Then he asked Mandy to pass him some antiseptic swabs and dressings.

Mr Western patted Boris's head as the dog gave a faint yelp of pain. 'Just wait until I get my hands on whoever did this!' he muttered.

Mandy thought she had never seen Mr Western looking so pale and shaken. Whatever his faults, he was certainly fond of his dog.

Once Boris was more comfortable, Sam Western turned to Mr Hope. 'I think it could have been poachers who shot Boris,' he said abruptly.

'What makes you think that?' asked Mr Hope.

'The shots I heard came from deep in the woods,' Sam Western replied. 'Farmers shoot rabbits out in the open. I'd have thought of it earlier if I hadn't been so worried about Boris.'

'Poachers!' Mandy threw a horrified glance at James.

James looked equally shaken by the news.

'It's certainly a possibility,' said Adam Hope. He looked across at Mandy and James. 'Did you two see anything suspicious when you were up here taking photographs this afternoon? Any people you didn't recognise?'

Mandy shook her head. 'No. We didn't see anyone, did we, James?'

'Just the Dalmatian,' answered James.

'Poachers are hardly going to advertise themselves though,' Sam Western said shortly.

Poachers! Horrible images of animals being hunted crowded Mandy's head. And what about the deer? Would they be all right? The thought of beautiful gentle Sprite or Honey-Mum lying dead was unbearable.

'I think you're going to need hard evidence that it was poachers before you alert the authorities,' Adam Hope warned Mr Western.

'Well, it's pretty obvious what happened, isn't it?' Sam Western replied. 'Boris got in someone's way when they were shooting at my deer. Why else would anyone be deep in the woods with rifles?'

'I'd say you were probably right,' Adam Hope said reasonably. 'But I don't think we can be certain at this stage.'

Mandy's head came up. As her dad said, there was no proof that it was poachers who had injured Boris. She had a sudden idea. 'Dad? Do you need me to help you any more?'

'No, you're all right,' Adam Hope answered. 'Mr

Western can help me put Boris into the back of the Land-rover.'

'So James and I have got time to have a quick look around?' Mandy asked.

Mr Hope took a look at his daughter's determined face. 'OK. But be careful and you'll have to be quick. I want to get Boris back to the unit pretty soon.'

'OK, Dad.' Mandy sprang towards the Land-rover. 'Come on,' she called to James.

'Where are we going?' James raised his eyebrows.

'To get some torches from the Land-rover. Dad always keeps some for night call-outs.' She found the torches and passed one to James. 'If it *was* poachers who shot Boris they might have left some signs.'

It was dark under the trees, away from the car headlights. Overhead, the first stars were out. Somewhere in the forest an owl hooted.

Mandy and James shone the powerful torches on to the ground. Twigs crunched beneath their trainers as they looked around.

'Seen anything yet?' Mandy whispered.

James shook his head. 'Just a few fir cones and some toadstools.'

'What we need is to find where Boris was shot,'

Mandy decided. 'Maybe we'll find an empty cartridge or something.'

'Good thinking. Hang on.' James paused briefly and began working things through logically. 'Look – Western parked over there, OK? He told us that Boris came running from that direction. So I reckon that it has to be somewhere around here that Boris was injured.'

'Sounds good to me,' Mandy said, swinging her torch.

The powerful beam of yellow light played over the moss-covered logs and patches of nettles. Taking small steps, Mandy quickly worked her way around the small clearing. Then she saw something glinting in a pile of leaves. 'James, over here!' she called excitedly. 'I think I've found something!'

'What is it?' James hurried over to her side as Mandy crouched down.

Mandy brushed the damp leaves aside and her fingers closed over a blue plastic tube with a metal cap at the closed end. An empty gun cartridge!

'Look!' She held it up for James to see.

James swung his torch in an arc over a nearby patch of leaves. He gave a cry of triumph. 'There are more of them over here.'

'This is the proof Mr Western needs!' Mandy

slipped the empty cartridges into the pocket of her jeans.

'Not exactly.' James frowned. 'It proves that someone has been firing a gun, but Sam Western already said that a farmer might have been shooting rabbits or something.'

'Oh, yes.' Mandy's face fell. 'And he sells permits for people to shoot pigeons on his estate, doesn't he?'

James nodded. 'If we want to prove that these were deer poachers we need to find some more evidence.'

'Like what?'

'Like . . . that!' Suddenly James leaped forward. 'Look over there!'

Mandy shone her torch in the direction James had indicated. The impressions were marked in the dark soft ground. Tyre tracks.

'These are really clear!' Mandy went and stood beside James. 'And footprints, too. More than two men. You can see the different patterns of the boots.'

'You would need a van for poaching large animals,' James pointed out.

Mandy shivered. It looked as if their worst suspicions might be confirmed.

'Let's go back and tell your dad and Sam Western,' said James.

Mandy and James emerged into the car park to find that Boris was safely in the back of the Land-rover.

'It looks like Mr Western was right about poachers,' Mandy said to her dad. 'We found these!' She held out the empty cartridges.

'And there are tyre marks and lots of footprints back there,' added James. 'It looks like there were three or four men.'

'Good work, you two,' said Adam Hope.

'Right,' Sam Western said grimly. 'I'd better stay and have a scout round here. I want to have a closer look at the evidence.'

'If you take my advice, you'll get some back-up,' said Mr Hope.

'Don't worry, I will. I'll call Dennis and get him to bring a couple of men over here.' Dennis Saville was Sam Western's estate manager. 'Make sure you look after Boris,' Mr Western added gruffly. 'Money's no object. I want him to have the best treatment.'

'All our patients get the best treatment,' Mandy was stung into replying.

Her dad put a hand on her shoulder. 'It's

all right, love,' he said softly.

Sam Western ignored Mandy's outburst. 'I'll call
in to check on Boris in the morning,' he said
shortly. He turned on his heel and strode away.
Then he stopped and looked back for a moment.
'Er – well done, both of you,' he said grudgingly
to Mandy and James.

'Coming from Sam Western, that's praise
indeed!' said Adam Hope with a broad grin as he
opened the Land-rover's door.

Mandy shrugged. She didn't care about being
thanked. She just hoped that the poachers would
be caught. Then Honey-Mum, Sprite, and the
other deer would be safe.

The journey home passed swiftly on the empty
roads, and shortly Adam Hope drew up in Welford
village. James got out and went towards his house.
'Thanks for the lift, Mr Hope. See you tomorrow,
Mandy,' he called.

It was completely dark by the time Adam Hope
pulled into the Hopes' front drive, past the
wooden sign which read, 'Animal Ark, Veterinary
Surgery'. He opened the car's back door and
reached for Boris who was wrapped snugly in a
blanket. 'Oof! This is one heavy dog,' he groaned.

'I'll help,' Mandy said.

Boris gave a rumbling growl and snapped at the air.

'Watch your fingers,' warned Mandy's dad.

They made their way carefully around to the red brick surgery attached to the back of the cottage.

Emily Hope popped her head round the door. Her curly red hair was tied back and she wore a fleece top, loose trousers, and trainers. 'Hello! I saw you arrive from the window. Isn't that one of Sam Western's dogs?'

'Hi, Mum!' Mandy said. 'Yes, it's Boris. Have you got a yoga class?'

'Yes. I was just leaving,' answered Emily Hope. She held the door open so that Mandy and Adam Hope could carry the dog inside.

'So how is it that you and James go out taking photographs and come back with a bulldog?' Mrs Hope asked.

While Boris was settled gently on the treatment room table, Mandy told her mum about Boris getting shot and the evidence she and James had found.

'Poachers? That's bad news.' Emily Hope grew serious as she listened.

Mr Hope nodded in agreement. 'These gangs are pretty organised nowadays. A lot of them are town based. Western's going to have his work cut out trying to track them down.'

'I expect he'll have notified the police by now,' said Emily Hope. 'Do you need a hand with Boris?'

Adam Hope shook his head. 'No. It's all right. Mandy can help me. You go to your class.'

'OK. If you're sure.' Mrs Hope dropped a brief kiss on Mandy's head. 'See you two later.'

In the treatment room, Adam Hope scrubbed his hands at the sink. Boris was trying to move around in his blanket.

'Poor boy,' Mandy soothed. 'Dad will soon make you better.'

Boris answered with a deep growl.

Mandy's dad reached into a cupboard. 'I'm just going to give this grumpy chap a bit more sedative before we see to him.'

'Good idea,' Mandy said. 'Isn't it a shame that injured animals don't always understand that we're trying to help them?'

Her dad nodded. 'It would certainly be useful to talk to the animals sometimes! Right,' Adam Hope went on, 'Boris is nice and relaxed now. I'll do the X-rays.'

There was a short wait while the X-rays were developed. Then Adam Hope pinned them up and switched on the light box. Mandy could see Boris's short strong leg bones, surrounded by about ten small white marks. 'Are those the pellets?' she pointed.

'Yes,' answered her dad. 'See how they've lodged in the muscles and missed the bone and major blood vessels? Boris is a very lucky dog.'

'Will his legs be all right?' Mandy asked.

'They should be. He's a strong healthy dog. But those are nasty wounds. I'll want to keep an eye on him for a day or two. Now, let's remove those pellets.'

Mandy washed her hands while her dad worked on Boris. Carefully, she took instruments from the sterilising unit and handed them to him.

'There. That's the last one,' Adam Hope said finally, straightening up. He opened the long, blunt-ended tweezers and the pellet clanged into a metal dish.

Mandy stroked Boris's wrinkled forehead. He was breathing deeply now and making loud rattling snorts.

'Isn't he noisy?' Mandy said, as her dad finished dressing Boris's wounds. 'He's going to keep all the other animals in the unit awake!'

'Bulldogs tend to snore loudly,' said Adam Hope, removing his rubber gloves. 'It's because they have pushed-back jaws and snub noses.'

Mandy's eyes sparkled. 'So what's your excuse for snoring, Dad?'

'Cheek!' Adam Hope pretended to look hurt. 'There's no respect for the older generation these days . . .' he added mournfully.

Mandy laughed and gave him an affectionate dig in the ribs.

'Boris is going to need a course of antibiotics,' said her dad, unlocking the medication cupboard.

'Not tablets, surely?' Mandy queried. She didn't envy anyone trying to get tablets down Boris's throat.

Mr Hope chuckled at the look on her face. 'Don't worry. I'll give him an injection now, then he can have drops in his food.'

'Phew! That's a relief,' Mandy said. 'Shall I help you settle him in the unit?'

Together they lifted the heavy, sleepy bulldog and took him through to the residential unit at the back of the extension. It smelt faintly of lemon disinfectant.

Mandy spread a cosy blanket in an empty cage. Then she filled a water bowl. 'There, Boris,' she said softly. 'You'll feel much better when you wake up.'

The only reply was a loud snore.

Mandy checked that the other animals had clean bedding, food and water. As she finally headed for the Animal Ark kitchen she realised that she was really hungry. It had been an eventful day, what with the deer, then Boris and the poachers . . . and then there had been the Dalmatian, too. With everything else, Mandy had almost forgotten about her.

Now Mandy began to worry again. Had the nervous dog found her way home? Or was she spending the night alone out on the bleak, dark moors? Mandy shivered. She didn't like the thought of that – especially not now there was the added danger of poachers.

Three

'Supper's ready!' Adam Hope lifted two steaming dishes out of the oven. 'There's garlic bread too.'

Mandy ground black pepper on to the tomato salad she had just made, then sat down at the table.

'Just what the doctor ordered.' Mr Hope began dishing out macaroni cheese.

'Don't you mean just what the vet ordered?' Mandy joked.

As they began to eat, Emily Hope came in. 'Mmm. It smells wonderful in here. All that yoga has given me an appetite.'

'I thought yoga was supposed to relax you,' Mandy said.

'That's right,' said her mum with a grin, her freckles seeming to dance across her nose. She sat down next to Mandy. 'I'm relaxed and starving.'

They all laughed.

'How's Boris?' asked Mrs Hope.

Her husband swallowed his mouthful of food before answering. 'He's resting in the unit. Mandy was pretty impressed by his loud snores, weren't you, love?'

'Uh-huh,' Mandy murmured absently, her mind back on the Dalmatian. She had only eaten a few mouthfuls and was now pushing the food around on her plate.

Emily Hope tapped Mandy's arm gently. 'Come on. Out with it.'

'What?' Mandy looked up in surprise.

'Whatever's on your mind,' her mum prompted.

'I think I know what it is,' said Mr Hope. 'You're still worried about that Dalmatian, aren't you?'

'Dalmatian?' Emily Hope blinked. 'Correct me if I'm wrong, but I thought we were just talking about a bulldog!'

Mandy couldn't help laughing at her mum's puzzled expression. 'We were! But before we found out about Boris, James and I saw a Dalmatian running around the forest, all by herself. She seemed really nervous and I think her leg was injured.'

'Mandy persuaded me to drive around looking for her but we couldn't see any sign,' Mr Hope put in. 'I feel pretty sure that she's been reunited with her owner by now.'

'But you don't agree?' Emily Hope asked her daughter.

'No. Not really,' Mandy admitted. 'There was something a bit unusual about that dog.' She bit her lip, not sure how to explain why she felt so worried. 'She seemed so . . . spooked.'

'You're sure your imagination's not just working overtime?' Emily Hope asked gently.

Mandy blushed. She knew that she had a tendency to leap to conclusions sometimes, especially where animals were concerned. 'I don't think so. But I'll feel better when James and I have been back up to Glisterdale to look for her again tomorrow . . .' She tailed off, having caught the look that passed between her parents.

'I don't think that's a good idea,' said her mum. 'I'd rather you kept right away from those woods until the poachers have been caught.'

'Oh, Mum . . .' Mandy groaned. She cast a pleading glance at her father. Sometimes she could get round him more easily.

But he shook his head too. 'I'm afraid I agree with your mother. It's just too dangerous. You've seen what's happened to Boris.'

Mandy opened her mouth to speak.

'No buts, Mandy,' Emily Hope said firmly. 'I want you to promise that you'll stay away from those woods.'

'OK. I promise.' Mandy's shoulders slumped. She knew when she was beaten.

After supper, she helped clear and wash the dishes. Then she decided to go up to her bedroom. She had a bit more to do on her holiday homework and the new term started in a few days.

'Need any help with your small mammals project?' asked her mum.

'No thanks,' Mandy replied. 'I've just got a few pictures left to do.'

'All right,' Emily Hope looked concerned. 'See you later then. And try not to worry about that Dalmatian.' She gave Mandy a warm understanding smile.

Mandy went upstairs and pushed back the door to her room. She loved its low ceiling and the

thick dark beam running across it. She felt herself
relax as she began setting out paper and coloured
pencils.

For an hour she sat at the table by the window
and enjoyed making a detailed drawing of a field
mouse. A few last delicate strokes to the fur and it
was finished. She held up the drawing and sighed.
The mouse's head was wonky and its eyes looked
slightly crossed. 'It's not brilliant, but it's not too
bad,' she muttered, pulling a face.

After tidying away her pencils, she went
downstairs to say goodnight to her parents. She
found them in the sitting room. Her mum was
sitting by the fireplace, reading a vet's magazine,
while her dad was watching TV.

' 'Night, Mum. 'Night, Dad,' said Mandy.

'Goodnight,' replied her parents. 'Sleep tight.'

It was warm and cosy under her duvet, but
Mandy lay awake for a long time, thinking about
deer and poachers and an exhausted Dalmatian,
foot-sore and weary, spending a lonely night out
on the dales.

'OK. I give in,' said Mr Hope first thing the
following morning.

'What?' Mandy frowned.

'I know what those dark circles under your eyes mean, Mandy Hope,' Adam Hope went on. 'So if you and James want to go up to Glisterdale to look for that Dalmatian again, it's all right with me and your Mum.'

'Really?' Mandy flew across the kitchen to give him a hug. 'Thanks, Dad. That's brilliant!'

'Not so fast.' Emily Hope popped her head around the kitchen door. 'There is one condition.'

'Oh!' Mandy's face fell. That sounded like trouble.

'You have to take me with you,' her mum said, her eyes sparkling.

'Great! I can't think of a better way to spend a Sunday morning!' Mandy danced on the spot.

'And you have to do your usual chores first,' Adam Hope added, trying to sound strict.

'I'm already on my way,' Mandy sang out, halfway through the door. 'I'll just give James a ring first to tell him we'll pick him up!'

In the unit, Boris's muscular body was slumped in one corner. His bandaged back legs stuck out awkwardly. He gave a gruff complaining bark when Mandy went up to him.

'Poor you. Still feeling sore?' Mandy said

sympathetically. To her surprise Boris wagged his stumpy rosette of a tail. She felt bold enough to put a finger through the wire mesh and scratch his wrinkled forehead. Boris watched her for a few seconds. Then his black eyes narrowed and he gave a soft growl.

'OK, I get the message,' Mandy said, moving away. She usually reckoned she could get on with any animal, but Boris looked like being the exception.

She quickly filled water and food bowls and changed litter trays. The important work over, she set about wiping surfaces and mopping the floor at double speed.

'Finished!' she declared. 'Time for Operation Dalmatian!' Dashing through into the cottage, she went to find her boots and anorak.

'All things bright and beautiful . . .' Adam Hope sang out.

Mandy grimaced as she darted out to the front drive. 'Have a good choir practice, Dad! See you later.'

'By-eee!' came the long deep note.

Mandy climbed in beside her mum and they went to pick up James.

The roads were clear, and it wasn't long before Mrs Hope was driving the Land-rover up the winding road across the moors. Strands of grey mist hung low around the fields, bleaching the colours from the trees and hedges.

'OK. Over to you two. Where do we start looking for this elusive Dalmatian?' asked Emily Hope.

Mandy gave her mum directions. 'Last time we saw it, it was hurtling through the woods up near Upper Welford Hall.'

Mrs Hope shifted the car's gears. 'The woods it is, then.'

Mandy kept her eyes peeled for any sign of the Dalmatian. She felt herself grow tense as they reached the woods where Boris had been shot. She peered anxiously into the trees at the side of the road. Glancing in the car's mirror, she saw that James looked worried too.

But there was no sign of any gang of men with guns, and no sign of a lone dog either.

'Maybe we should widen the search,' suggested Emily Hope after an hour of fruitless driving through the forest. 'Shall we try looking on the moors?'

Mandy and James agreed. As her mum drove on, Mandy's eyes roved over every bare ridge, and every stretch of stony hillside. The moors were covered with stunted grass and tough, spiky gorse. 'There's nowhere here for a dog to shelter,' she pointed out. She tried to imagine what she would do if she were a dog. Where would she go to find warmth and shelter? A barn? A stable? Well, a farm had those things. 'I think we should check out any farms,' she decided.

James pointed down to the valley bottom. A cluster of grey buildings nestled there behind some trees. 'That's the first one we've seen.'

'Let's try it then.' Mrs Hope steered the Land-rover into the farmyard and stopped outside the farmhouse. 'We'd better go and ask if it's OK for us to look around.'

She got out and went to knock on the door. Mandy and James went with her. A man answered almost at once.

'Good morning. We're looking for a Dalmatian. Have you seen one?' Emily Hope asked the farmer.

'No, haven't seen anything on four legs around here except my sheep. But you're welcome to look around,' the farmer said. 'I hope you find your dog.'

'Oh, it's not our dog,' Mandy said.

'We think it might be a stray,' James added.

'Oh, aye. Well good luck anyway.' The farmer nodded to them and went back inside.

Mandy, her mum and James looked round the farmyard. They checked the barns, feed sheds and garages, but there was nothing. Mandy let out a discouraged sigh and put her hands on her hips, gazing out across the fields.

Where else was there to look? Suddenly she caught sight of an old stone barn. There were holes in the roof and the door hung off its hinges

at an awkward angle. 'I'm going to look over there!' she called to James and her mum.

Her feet pounded against the grass as she ran. As she reached the barn, she slowed down and went quietly inside. She breathed in the scent of dust, dried leaves and old straw. Daylight shining in through holes in the roof illuminated the dusky gloom.

Wooden pens stood against the far wall. Mandy looked more closely. What was that? It looked as though there was something curled up tight in one of them. Now it was looking at her with wide scared eyes.

It was the Dalmatian!

'Oh!' Mandy breathed. 'We've found you at last!'

She bent down to make herself seem smaller and less threatening as she began moving slowly towards the frightened dog. 'Hello, again. You must be hungry and cold,' she murmured.

The Dalmatian kept her eyes on Mandy's face. She licked her lips nervously and rose unsteadily to her feet.

Mandy's mum and James appeared in the doorway. Mandy looked over her shoulder and signalled to them not to make any sudden moves. She could see by their faces that they understood.

'Take care, Mandy,' Emily Hope said a low voice. 'She seems very scared.'

Mandy nodded. She knew that dogs could sometimes bite in fear as well as in anger.

The Dalmatian stood there trembling. It stared into her face as she held her hand out for it to sniff.

'It's OK, we're here to help you,' she said softly. Mandy held her breath. For a moment, she thought that the dog was going to run away again, then its long tail began to wag and a cold nose brushed against her fingers.

'It's all right! She wants to be friends,' she called over her shoulder to her mum and James. 'Aren't you a sweetheart?' she added as she stroked the dog's muscular chest.

James and Mrs Hope came over and crouched down next to Mandy.

'Isn't she lovely?' James fondled the Dalmatian's spotted ears. But as his hand brushed against the dog's head, she whined and drew back.

Emily Hope frowned. 'It looks like she has some tenderness there. And she seems unsteady on her feet. Keep talking to her, Mandy. I'll check her over.'

Mandy and James watched as Mrs Hope examined the dog.

'Oh,' Mandy gasped, when her mum lifted one of the dog's feet. 'Her pads are all cracked and sore.'

Mrs Hope nodded. 'She's covered a long distance on those. But they'll soon heal. I'm more puzzled by this lump on her head. It seems to be an older injury.'

'How could she have hurt her head?' asked James.

'It's hard to say without knowing anything about her,' replied Emily Hope. 'I'll have a closer look when we get her back to Animal Ark. But just now I want to give her some fluids. She's very dehydrated.'

Mandy nipped back to the Land-rover to fetch her mum's bag. 'There we are,' said Mrs Hope, giving the dog an injection. 'That'll make you feel better. Now, let's get you back to the surgery and on to a drip.'

Just then a voice came floating into the barn. It was a girl calling out a name, over and over again. 'Echo! Echo!' The voice cracked on a sob. 'Oh, Echo! Where are you?'

Mandy and James looked at each other. 'You don't think she's looking for this Dalmatian, do you?' said James.

'Let's go and see!' Mandy urged.

They leaped to their feet and ran over to the open barn door. Just as they reached it, a girl came running up. She looked about thirteen. Her face was white and tear-stained.

Then Mandy saw her catch sight of Mrs Hope kneeling down next to the exhausted dog. The girl gave a trembling smile and her whole face seemed to light up with relief.

'Echo!' she breathed. 'It really is you. Where have you been?'

Four

Mandy watched as the girl ran straight over and threw her arms round the Dalmatian's neck. 'I've been so worried about you,' she murmured. Echo gave a short bark and licked her owner's face.

'She seems really pleased to see you,' Mandy said.

'Yes. She does, doesn't she?' The girl beamed and dried her eyes. She had long dark hair and an open friendly face. 'I'm Julia Hampton,' she said. 'And Echo's my dog. She ran off while we were out for a walk,' she explained, stroking the Dalmatian's ears over and over.

Mandy liked Julia at once. 'Hi, I'm Mandy

Hope,' she said. 'And this is James Hunter.'

'Hi,' said James.

Julia seemed to notice the open vet's bag on the floor for the first time. She glanced at Emily Hope in alarm.

'My mum and dad are vets,' Mandy explained quickly. 'Mum was just giving Echo some emergency treatment.'

Julia's face fell. 'Is something wrong with Echo?'

'Nothing that we can't fix,' Mrs Hope said reassuringly. 'She's exhausted and dehydrated and those sore paws are going to need some attention, but we'll soon have her right.'

The strained look was fading from around Julia's eyes. 'Thank you so much for finding Echo and looking after her.'

'You have Mandy and James here to thank for that,' said Emily Hope. 'They saw your dog running on the dales yesterday and were worried about who she belonged to. The two of them wouldn't give up until we had searched every last bit of Glisterdale.'

'Really?' Julia looked surprised and grateful. She turned to Mandy and James. 'That's brilliant.'

'That's OK,' they answered. James, shy as usual, blushed.

Emily Hope laughed. 'Once you get to know these two, you'll understand. They never give up if they think an animal needs rescuing.'

'Lucky for me and Echo then!' said Julia. 'I don't really know what happened yesterday. I was taking Echo for a walk on the moors when she ran away. I called her and called her, but she didn't come back. She's run off once before, but this is the first time she's stayed out all night.'

'Sounds like Echo needs a few obedience lessons,' Emily Hope said gently. 'Has she always been like that?'

Julia shook her head. 'No. She used to be so lovely and good-natured. Mum used to say that she was my shadow – she went everywhere with me. But now she seems so jumpy all the time. She even snapped at me the other day.'

'But Echo seems like such a lovely gentle dog,' Mandy said.

'She soon made friends with us, didn't she?' James added.

Mandy nodded. 'And she must have been in pain as well as feeling scared and confused, but she didn't snap or anything.'

'That's true, love,' her mum said thoughtfully. She looked at Julia. 'How odd that Echo's temperament has changed so drastically. It must be very difficult for you and your family.'

'It is!' Julia's eyes filled with tears. 'Mum and Dad are fed up with her running away and being so nervous and snappy. They want to find her a new home.'

'Oh, no!' Mandy felt really sorry for Julia. She obviously loved Echo and wanted to keep her pet.

Mrs Hope gave Julia a tissue. She patted her arm. 'Things might not be as bad as they look. They rarely are. Come on, I'd like to get Echo back to Animal Ark – that's our veterinary surgery. You should come too.'

'I'll have to tell my parents where I am,' said Julia. 'We live near here. They know I'm looking for Echo, but they'll be worried if I'm back late.'

'That's OK. You can use Mum's mobile to call your parents,' Mandy suggested. 'Couldn't she, Mum?'

Mrs Hope nodded. 'Of course. Tell them that you can come in the Land-rover with Echo. Maybe they could meet you at Animal Ark?'

'OK. Thanks.' Julia made her call, then she handed the mobile back to Emily Hope, her expression downcast. 'They said they'll meet me at the surgery.'

'What's wrong?' Mandy asked.

Julia shrugged. She looked up at Mandy, her face white and set. 'Mum and Dad didn't say anything, but I can tell they're not too thrilled that I've found Echo. She's just too much trouble, you see? They probably wish that Echo had run off and had never come back!'

Back at Animal Ark, the Hamptons had driven over to meet their daughter. They stood with sombre expressions in the treatment room, where Echo lay on the table.

As Mrs Hope treated Echo, Julia stroked the Dalmatian.

'Be careful, Julia. Echo might snap at you,' Mrs Hampton warned her daughter. Mandy thought Julia's mum sounded more worried about Echo than annoyed.

But the strong muscular dog only licked her owner's hand gently. 'She's fine now, Mum,' Julia smiled.

Mandy frowned. It was hard to believe that this was the same problem dog Julia had described.

'Hmm. I'm still puzzled by that lump on her head,' said Mrs Hope. 'It seems sore, but there's no broken skin, so I think I'll leave well alone.'

She went over to the sink to wash her hands. 'Echo's much calmer after the sedative I've given her and her paws will feel a lot more comfortable soon. But she's still very dehydrated. I'd like to keep her here on a drip overnight.'

'Is that OK?' Julia asked her parents.

'Of course it is, darling,' said Julia's mum. 'Echo means the world to you, doesn't she?' Mrs Hampton gave her daughter a hug. She had brown hair like Julia's, but worn short and spiky.

Julia glared at her mother and pulled away. 'So why do you want to find her a new home?' she demanded.

Mrs Hampton looked a little uncomfortable. 'You know we don't want to do that, love. But if Echo keeps running off and being so unpredictable, we might have no choice.'

Julia tossed her dark hair over her shoulder. She seemed about to protest again.

'I find it's better not to make these kind of decisions in haste,' Emily Hope said quickly, in her warm sensible way. 'Why don't we wait and see how Echo is after a day or so?'

Julia gave her a grateful smile. 'OK.'

'That's a very good idea,' Mr Hampton agreed.

'And don't worry about Echo,' Mandy said to

Julia. 'I'll make sure she's all right.'

'Mandy keeps an eye on all the patients in the residential unit,' Mrs Hope explained.

Echo gave a soft bark and wagged her tail.

'She's saying that she feels a lot better,' Julia said confidently, running a hand over Echo's head.

Mr and Mrs Hampton managed a smile but Mandy could see that they still looked worried. Julia gave Echo a final cuddle, then left for home with her parents.

'What's that terrible noise?' James followed Mandy and Emily Hope, as they led Echo through to the unit.

Loud rumbling sounds filled the spotless room which was lined with wire cages. In one of them a squat white shape lay flat on its tummy, with its front legs sticking out straight. Boris!

Mandy chuckled. 'That's him – snoring!'

James looked impressed. 'Wow! I bet that would register on a decibel meter!'

'A what?' Mandy said, puzzled.

'A machine that measures sound levels,' said James.

'Poor old Echo is never going to get any rest with that noise,' Mandy observed.

'Or any other patient either!' Mrs Hope said with a smile as another rattling snore filled the air.

Mandy and James chuckled. 'You have to see the funny side!' Mandy pointed out.

She helped make Echo comfortable in a large cage. Echo turned round a couple of times, then curled up on the clean blanket. She put her nose between her paws and seemed to fall asleep straight away.

'Amazing!' Mandy said. 'She must be really exhausted if not even that racket can disturb her.'

Just then a familiar figure in a tweed jacket appeared at the entrance to the unit. It was Sam Western. 'The back door was open,' he said. 'I know the surgery is closed on Sundays, but I thought I'd just look in on Boris.'

'Come in, Mr Western,' Mrs Hope said warmly.

Sam Western came over to Boris's cage. 'How is he doing?'

'He's a bit sore and still groggy from the medication, but he's going to be fine,' said Mrs Hope. 'Luckily the pellets didn't do too much damage.'

'Ah, well. He's a strong healthy dog,' Sam Western said proudly.

'And bad-tempered and very noisy . . .' James whispered so that only Mandy could hear. Mandy's lips twitched.

Boris roused as he heard his owner's voice. Lifting his head, he gave a sleepy bark.

Mrs Hope opened the cage so that Sam Western could stroke Boris.

'Good lad,' Sam Western said fondly, scratching Boris behind the ears. Boris opened his jaws to give his owner a fierce doggy grin.

'Look at those teeth!' James muttered to Mandy.

Mandy nodded. 'I wouldn't give much for anyone else's chances of stroking Boris!' She waited until Boris's cage was locked once again, then said, 'Is there any news about the poachers, Mr Western?'

'Not so far, but I've told the police about the cartridges you found, and the tyre tracks,' Sam Western answered. 'It seems that there have been a few incidents round here during the past few weeks.'

'Do you think it's an organised set-up?' asked Mrs Hope.

'It could be,' replied Sam Western. 'The police seem to think so too. They're making enquiries, but these people are always hard to catch.'

'So, what about the deer?' Mandy said, unable to stop herself from speaking out. 'Are they still in danger?'

Sam Western gave her a hard look. 'You can be sure that I'm taking steps to protect my property. Dennis is organising security patrols during the night.'

Mandy knew that she could never think of the deer as property, but she was glad about the night patrols. Honey-Mum and Sprite would at least have some protection.

'That's a wise precaution,' agreed Mrs Hope. 'Poaching is a nasty business.'

Sam Western nodded shortly. 'It's not just the killing and stealing. Poachers aren't fussy about injuring animals. They damage a lot of stock, and I've spent good time and money managing the herd.'

Mandy opened her mouth, but at a look from her mum shut it again.

'Well, let's hope the police find the culprits before they do any more harm,' Mrs Hope said firmly.

'I can't argue with that,' Sam Western answered. 'Now, when can I take Boris home?'

'Oh, he'll be fine in a couple of days,' said Emily

Hope. 'Either myself or Adam will give you a ring to tell you when he can be collected.'

'Well, thanks,' Sam Western nodded and left to go about his business.

Mandy gave an explosive sigh. 'All that horrible man cares about is how much money he's going to lose because of poachers!' she said angrily. 'He doesn't care about animals at all!'

'Calm down, Mandy,' her mother said. 'Sam Western's a hard-headed sort, I grant you. But he did agree to leave the ancient woodland alone when he bought the wood, remember? And that meant he safeguarded the deer's home.'

'I suppose so,' Mandy said reluctantly.

'And you can't deny that he's fond of Boris.' Emily Hope put her arm round her daughter's shoulder and gave her a quick hug. 'Things are never simply black and white in this world,' she said.

'They are for Echo!' joked James.

'Oh, ha ha! Trust you, James Hunter!' Mandy said.

'Very good, James.' Mrs Hope chuckled. 'Now, who's for a nice cup of tea? There's some of your grandma's cake to go with it.'

'Great!' said James.

Mandy grinned as they all headed for the kitchen. James loved her gran's cooking.

Adam Hope arrived back from choir practice just as the kettle boiled. He looked at the rich fruitcake and plate of sticky flapjacks and rubbed his hands together. 'Lovely. Just the job!' he said, pouring a cup of tea.

Mandy couldn't wait to fill her dad in on all the details about finding Echo in the barn. And then there was Sam Western's visit. Between sips of tea, and helped by James, she told him everything.

'Well, you have been busy,' said Mr Hope, when Mandy and James had finished. He turned to his wife. 'It sounds like it hasn't been a very relaxing Sunday for you.'

Emily Hope shrugged. 'It couldn't be helped. But I was hoping to get some paperwork done before that vet's conference next week.'

Mandy swallowed a last mouthful of flapjack and jumped to her feet. 'Why don't James and I do the feeding in the unit this evening? Then you can do your paperwork. We don't mind, do we, James?'

James shook his head. 'No problem.'

Mrs Hope pushed back a stray red curl. 'Thanks, you two. That would be a great help.'

Mandy led the way to the feed cupboard in the unit. Inside, the shelves were stocked with tins and packets of every description. There was cat food, dog food, rabbit food, bird seed and food for animals on special diets.

'OK,' Mandy said, getting organised. She took down some tins of cat and dog food and a bag of rabbit food, then stacked them all on the food preparation counter at one side of the unit.

'I'll get some dishes down,' said James. He reached up to a shelf above the counter. As he took them down, the pile of clean metal bowls slid sideways. 'Whoops!'

James tried his best to catch them. Too late. They crashed to the ground with a tremendous noise.

Boris shot to his feet and began barking loudly. The kitten howled, her fur standing on end.

'Oh, no,' James said sheepishly. The noise was dreadful.

Mandy grinned. 'Never mind,' she called out. 'They'll settle down again in a minute.'

As she bent down to help pick up the bowls, her gaze fell on Echo's cage. Echo was awake, but still curled up on her blanket. She stared out placidly, her deep-brown eyes calm and untroubled.

'That's odd,' Mandy said, frowning. 'I thought Julia said Echo was jumpy.'

'She did.' James stacked the metal bowls on the counter.

'So how come Echo was so calm when those bowls crashed down and with Boris and the kitten making so much noise?' Mandy demanded.

James looked bemused. 'I don't know. It's weird, isn't it?'

Mandy fell silent, trying to puzzle it out. Then everything started to come clear. 'Unless . . . That's it! James! I think I might know what's wrong with Echo!'

Five

As soon as all the animals in the unit had been fed, Mandy hurried back into the cottage. James followed her into the study.

'Mum!' Mandy burst out excitedly. 'I think I know why Echo's so nervous. She can't help it. I think she's deaf – just like Maisy!'

Maisy was a beautiful Dalmatian with liver brown spots and amber eyes. She belonged to Elise Knight, who was a writer.

Emily Hope was sitting at Grandad's big old desk. She looked up from her notes with a patient smile. 'What's all this about Echo and Maisy?' she asked.

Mandy began again, more slowly this time. 'We were feeding the animals and James dropped a whole stack of dishes.'

'It made a terrific noise,' added James, blushing bright red. 'Boris went wild.'

'The other animals nearly jumped out of their skins too,' Mandy went on. 'Except for Echo!'

'And Julia already said that Echo won't come when she calls her,' James reminded Mrs Hope.

'So you put two and two together?' Mrs Hope said with a smile.

'Yes! And then we thought about Maisy!' Mandy said. It all seemed so clear now. 'Remember how Elise was worried because Maisy wasn't as lively and alert as she should have been for her age?'

'That's right,' said her mum. 'I ran some tests and found out that Maisy was deaf.'

'So you could run the same tests on Echo, couldn't you?' Mandy said. 'Then we'd know if my hunch was right.'

Mrs Hope nodded slowly. 'I've a feeling you could be on to something. I'll have a word with Julia and her parents when they call in tomorrow.'

'Couldn't you just take a quick look at her now?' Mandy pleaded. 'It wouldn't take long.'

Mrs Hope gave a long sigh. Then she stood up.

'Come on, then. I expect this paperwork can wait for another few minutes.'

'Thanks, Mum,' Mandy said, giving her a hug. 'You're a star!'

In the unit, Mandy opened Echo's cage. She reached in and gently scratched the top of Echo's head. She could still feel the slight lump there.

'Don't worry, Echo,' Mandy whispered. 'Mum is going to find out what's wrong with you.'

Echo looked alert and her tail wagged eagerly. But as soon as Mandy stopped looking directly at her, she seemed to lose interest. She lay down again and stared into space.

'She's acting just like Maisy did before Mum found out what was wrong,' Mandy said to James.

'Poor Echo,' said James. 'No wonder she seems jumpy and nervous.'

Emily Hope stayed at the side of the room out of Echo's line of vision. She snapped her fingers and called Echo's name. But Echo didn't look round. She just lay in her cage, her nose on her paws.

When Mrs Hope came back round to the front of her cage, Echo looked up at her. Her tail wagged slightly.

'Well, she certainly could have a hearing problem, but I think she's still too weak to run proper tests,' Mrs Hope concluded. 'And without them it's going to be difficult to be sure.'

'Oh.' Mandy felt disappointed. It looked like they were going to have to wait a bit longer before finding out if her theory was right. 'Thanks for looking at Echo again anyway.'

'No problem.' Mandy's mum ruffled her daughter's fair hair. 'I know you and James are eager to get to the bottom of this. 'Now – I really have to catch up with those notes!' She went out of the unit.

James had to go too. Mandy went to see him out.

'When do you think your mum will do the tests?' James asked at the front door.

'Probably in a day or two,' Mandy guessed. 'Julia and her parents are calling in tomorrow to collect Echo. I suppose she'll have to ask them if it's OK.'

James nodded. 'I have to go and buy a new school uniform with Mum tomorrow morning.' He pulled a face at the thought. 'But I'll meet you later.'

Mandy grinned. James hated going shopping for clothes. But if it had been for a computer or a new camera lens, he wouldn't have minded at all!

'Hi there. Welcome to the usual Monday chaos!' Simon, the practice nurse, called as Mandy came in from the unit the following morning. 'How are our patients today?' Simon wanted to know.

Mandy smiled. 'Boris is even more grumpy and snappy, which must mean he's feeling better! And Echo seems a lot stronger.'

'That's good.' Simon's eyes twinkled in a friendly fashion behind his wire-rimmed glasses. 'Your dad's just been called out to one of the farms. A cow has slipped and hurt her leg, so your mum and I are holding the fort.'

'I can help out. I'm not meeting James till later,' Mandy said.

'You're a real life-saver,' Simon grinned as he called out for the next patient to come through. 'See you later,' he said to Mandy, as he disappeared into one of the treatment rooms.

'Phew!' Mandy said. 'Simon wasn't joking about the chaos!' There was a long queue at reception. Every chair was occupied by owners, some with pet carriers, others with dogs on leads.

'So you'd better make an appointment for a week from today for a check-up. But that leg's doing fine.' Mandy's mum appeared at the door of the treatment room followed by Robbie Grimshaw and Biddy, his Welsh collie.

'Now, Reverend Hadcroft, if you'd like to bring Jemima in,' Emily Hope called to the next patient. She glanced round the packed waiting room and gave her daughter a grateful smile. 'Oh, good. I'm glad you're here to lend a hand, love.'

Mandy grinned. 'One down, fifty to go!' she joked as Reverend Hadcroft carried his cat in for treatment. She went across and slipped behind the reception desk. 'Who's next, please?' she asked politely.

Jean Knox, the grey-haired receptionist, flashed her a grateful glance. 'Thanks, Mandy. I've hardly had a moment to think since we opened. And I can't seem to find my glasses . . .' She plucked at her cardigan where her glasses usually hung on their chain.

Mandy hid a smile. Jean was really nice, but so absent-minded. 'They're on top of your head,' she whispered.

'Oh, thank you. Silly me.' Jean pulled her glasses on to her nose.

For the next half hour Mandy was kept busy handing out prescriptions and dealing with cheques. The queue gradually became smaller.

Suddenly the front door burst open and a woman rushed in. She was carrying a fluffy grey cat wrapped in a blanket. 'Can I see someone right away?' she asked in a shaky voice. 'Penny's been hit by a car!'

Emily Hope had just finished with a patient. She stepped forward and beckoned to the woman. 'Bring her straight through,' she said. 'Mandy, I could do with an extra pair of hands, please.'

Mandy leaped into action and followed the distressed woman into the treatment room. She helped keep Penny calm while her mum examined her. Luckily there were no broken bones.

When the woman had been given some pills to reduce the swelling, Mandy went back into reception. Julia and her parents were just arriving for their appointment.

'Hello,' Julia said with a bright smile. Her dark hair was drawn back into a pony-tail and she was wearing jeans and a yellow T-shirt. 'We've come to take Echo home.'

'I'm sure that's OK,' Mandy said. 'But I think Mum wants to have a word with you about her before she goes home.'

Julia's dark brows shot together. 'Why? What's wrong?' she asked.

'Oh, no. Now what?' said Julia's father under his breath.

'Here's Mrs Hope now,' Julia's mum said soothingly. 'Come on, let's all go and listen to what she has to say.'

'You know something, don't you?' Julia said to Mandy, when they were all in the unit.

Mandy nodded and glanced at her mum.

Emily Hope smiled. 'Go ahead, Mandy. Tell Julia and her parents what you and James have found out.'

Once again Mandy repeated the story of the dropped metal dishes and Echo's lack of reaction. 'And we know a gorgeous Dalmatian called Maisy, who had symptoms a bit like Echo's,' Mandy went on. 'Mum did some tests and found out that Maisy was deaf. So, anyway, I thought that Echo might be deaf too, like Maisy and because of the dishes. And then . . .'

'Deaf? But that isn't possible!' Julia's father interrupted.

'No way! Echo can't be deaf,' Julia agreed. She faced Mandy with her hands on her hips.

'But . . .' Mandy was taken aback by Julia's

certainty. 'How can you know for sure?'

'Because she was tested for deafness when she was a puppy. She passed all her tests with flying colours!' Julia said triumphantly. 'And, anyway, Echo was really easy to train when we first had her.'

'That's right,' Mr Hampton confirmed. 'She had a lovely nature. That's why we chose her over other pups in the litter. It's only been recently that there's been any problem with her.'

'Was there no sign of hearing loss at all?' asked Emily Hope.

'No.' Julia shook her head, so that her pony-tail bobbed about.

'Oh.' Mandy fell silent. This just didn't make sense. She glanced at her mum and saw that she was frowning.

'Well, Echo's certainly posing us a puzzle,' said Mrs Hope. 'I really thought Mandy and James were right.'

So did we, Mandy thought glumly.

'Is it OK if we take Echo home now?' Julia asked eagerly.

Mrs Hope smiled. 'I don't see why not. She'll be fine after a bit more rest. But I'd make sure you keep her on a lead, until you can be certain that she will come when you call her.'

'Oh.' Julia looked disappointed. 'What a shame. Echo loves running. She's really going to miss being out on the dales with me.'

'That can't be helped for now,' said Julia's mum. 'We don't want a repeat of this latest incident, do we?'

Julia shook her head, looking miserable. Then she brightened up. 'Anyway, it's brilliant to have Echo back, isn't it?'

Mandy couldn't help noticing that there was a slight hesitation before Julia's parents smiled and nodded.

Julia and Echo's problems are not over yet, she thought sadly.

After Julia had left with Echo, Mandy went back into reception. It was almost time for surgery to close. She began tidying up. The door opened and a pretty young woman with a Dalmatian on a lead came in. It was Elise Knight with Maisy. Mandy smiled broadly. What a coincidence!

'Hello, Mandy. Am I too late?' asked Elise. 'I just popped in to pick up some worming tablets for Maisy.'

'Hi, Elise,' Mandy said delightedly. 'No, it's OK.

There's ten minutes before we close. Shall I get the tablets, Jean?' she offered.

'Oh, would you, dear? Thanks.' Jean looked up from her computer. 'Hello, Elise. Maisy looks well.'

'She is, thanks,' answered Elise, looking down proudly at her dog. She stroked Maisy's head. The Dalmatian looked up at her with alert golden-brown eyes.

'How's the training going?' Mandy asked as she handed Elise the small packet.

'Maisy's doing brilliantly. Far better than I'd expected.' Elise smiled broadly as she counted out the money for the worming tablets. 'I can even let her off the lead for a run now. As soon as I blow her special whistle, she comes back straight away.' It had been Mrs Hope's idea that Maisy might be able to hear a high-pitched dog whistle. Mandy knew that humans couldn't hear the whistle, but animals could.

'That's great!' Mandy said. She came round the desk to say hello to Maisy. Making sure she was in the dog's line of sight, she slapped her hands on her knees in an eager 'come here' sign. Maisy's beautiful eyes lit up and she bounded across the room.

'Whoa!' Mandy laughed, staggering backwards,

as the Dalmatian jumped up at her. She rubbed her face against Maisy's head. 'Hello, gorgeous!'

Elise Knight laughed. 'That's one signal she has no problem with!' She touched Maisy's shoulder to get her attention. Then she pointed to the ground. 'That's enough fuss now. You'll push Mandy over!'

Maisy looked up at her owner, then sat down obediently.

'Clever girl.' Mandy patted and praised Maisy.

'You and James must take some of the credit,' said Elise. 'I don't think I'd have managed so well without your help.'

'That's OK,' Mandy said, feeling a bit embarrassed as she always did when people thanked her. 'We loved helping.' She knew that James would agree. She glanced down at Maisy, who was lying down with her nose on her paws. Mandy was struck by the way Maisy stared into space when no one was talking directly to her, just like Echo did. 'We had a Dalmatian here last night called Echo,' she told Elise. 'We thought she might be deaf too, like Maisy. Only she had all the tests at birth and they all came back clear.'

'Hmm, that does sounds puzzling,' Elise said. 'But if anyone can figure a problem out, it's your mum and dad. They're terrific vets!'

Mandy returned her smile. Elise was right. Her mum and dad were the best!

'I hope you find out what's wrong with Echo. Let me know if there's anything I can do,' Elise added.

'Thanks,' Mandy said. 'I will.'

'It's time we left,' said Elise. 'You must want to lock up. And Maisy is looking forward to her walk.' She bent down and ran her hand halfway down Maisy's back. Gently but firmly, she pressed her fingers into the dog's backbone.

Maisy stood up instantly, her tail wagging madly.

She turned her head and looked up at her owner. Elise took the dog's face in her hands to praise her. Then she made a walking movement with two fingers.

Maisy's tail wagged nineteen to the dozen. She whined eagerly.

'She certainly understood that,' Mandy said with a chuckle. 'You two are terrific.'

Elise smiled proudly. 'Maisy does all the hard work. She learns so quickly. I can't believe I was worried that I wouldn't cope at first. I don't know what I'd do without her now.'

'She is gorgeous.' Mandy bent down to give Maisy a hug, before Elise led her away. 'Bye,' she called. 'Take care!'

After surgery closed, she phoned James and arranged to meet him. She fetched her bike from the shed, then cycled down the lane. James was waiting for her at the Fox and Goose crossroads. 'How's Echo?' he asked straight away.

Mandy told him, then explained about Maisy and Elise calling into the surgery too. After she finished speaking, James looked puzzled. 'So there's no point in your mum doing those tests?'

'Doesn't seem like it,' Mandy said. 'Julia is certain that Echo can't be deaf.' She shrugged.

'It's still a mystery. Did you get your new uniform?'

James nodded. 'Everyone else was doing the same. It took ages . . .'

Mandy felt a laugh bubbling up at the disgusted look on his face.

'And now Mum's just remembered that she forgot to stock up with wild bird food,' James went on. 'Do you fancy cycling over to the pet shop in Walton?'

'Try and stop me!' Mandy said with a wide grin. She loved going to the pet shop.

They cycled along the narrow winding road across the moor. The recent winds had stripped many leaves from the trees. A wet carpet of red, yellow and russet lined the verges.

They propped up their bikes outside Piper's Pets in the main street. James bought two plastic bags of wild bird seed and a huge bag of peanuts. 'I'll get Blackie a treat too,' he said, picking up a bone-shaped dog biscuit.

On their way back through Welford, Mandy stopped off at James's house to say hello to Blackie. 'Hello, boy!' She patted his solid wriggling body as he came hurrying out to meet them. Blackie jumped up and licked her chin.

'Get down, Blackie!' James ordered, his face red.

'Push him off, Mandy. I'm trying to teach him not to jump up.' Blackie ignored James. He gave a short bark and pawed Mandy's jeans, asking for more fuss.

Mandy grinned. 'Blackie will get the idea – in about ten years' time! Never mind. He's still lovely!'

But she couldn't help but contrast the boisterous Labrador with poor nervous Echo. Something was definitely wrong with the Dalmatian. And there just had to be a way to find out what it was.

Six

A growl rumbled in Boris's throat as Mandy filled his water dish the following morning. His dark eyes glared out of his broad wrinkled face.

'And thank you to you too!' Mandy said dryly. Then she heard a chuckle behind her. She turned round and saw her father coming into the unit.

'You won't have to put up with this ungrateful patient much longer,' he said. 'He's well on the mend now. Time he went home.'

Mandy grinned. 'I reckon Boris likes everyone to think he's a hard case. But he's mad about me really!'

Adam Hope smiled. 'Sensible dog!' He ruffled

his daughter's hair. 'I'll go and phone Sam Western now. I have to make another call to High Cross Farm this morning. It's near Upper Welford Hall, so I can drop Boris off.'

'High Cross Farm? Is something else wrong with Lydia's goats?' Mandy was instantly concerned.

'No, nothing like that. I promised to take her a tin of vitamin powder, that's all. And a couple of other things . . .' Adam Hope tailed off.

I bet you're not charging her for them, Mandy thought. Her kind-hearted dad knew that Lydia Fawcett didn't have a lot of money. 'Can James and I get a lift with you?' she asked. 'We could stow our bikes on the roof rack and then go for a bike ride when we've dropped Boris off.'

'Sounds like you've got it all worked out,' observed her dad.

'I have!' Mandy said. 'We still want to get some photos for the competition. I'll phone James and tell him we'll pick him up!'

'Ah, that's right. You didn't manage to take many photos when you were last up at Glisterdale, did you?' remembered Adam Hope.

Mandy shook her head. 'We were too busy trying to find Echo, then poor old Boris was shot by the poachers.'

'Speaking of poachers, make sure you and James keep out of those woods,' Adam Hope warned.

'OK. We'll be careful,' Mandy promised. She felt the familiar sick feeling in her stomach at the thought of the poachers preying on the lovely fallow deer. She went to phone James, then came straight back.

'Right. All set?' Mr Hope rubbed his palms together. 'Shall we get our grumpy friend here into the Land-rover?'

'Grr-uff!' Boris blinked hopefully at them through the cage.

Mandy laughed. 'I think he knows he's going home!'

'Here we are.' Adam Hope drove the Land-rover through the big double gates. Gravel crunched beneath the tyres as they drew up in front of an imposing stone doorway with ivy around it.

Mandy glanced around. She had been to Upper Welford Hall a few times. The lawns were like green velvet, and every tree and bush was clipped into a precise shape. At the end of the lawn, there was an ornamental lake with Canada geese and weeping willows. 'It's all very nice,' she commented to James. 'But I'd rather have our own garden!'

James nodded in agreement. 'You wouldn't dare to walk on Mr Western's lawn in case you left a mark.'

Sam Western himself answered the front door. 'Ah, you've brought Boris back,' he said, looking pleased. He came round to the back of the Land-rover.

Adam Hope opened the boot and stood back to let Mr Western see his dog.

'Come on, old fellow.' Sam Western reached in and lifted Boris out. Boris whined, but didn't struggle. 'Can he walk?' Sam Western asked.

'Yes, but gently does it. No strenuous activity for a week or so.' Adam Hope watched as Sam Western placed his dog gently on the ground.

'Right you are. Thanks for dropping him off,' Sam Western said gruffly. 'Come on, Boris.'

Boris waddled awkwardly towards the open front door. Then he stopped and glanced over his shoulder. His round black eyes sought out Mandy and he gave a short bark, his crooked rosette of a tail wagging.

'Goodness! I think he just said thank you!' said James in amazement.

Mandy took a step forward, meaning to give Boris a farewell pat. But Boris growled and nipped into the house. Mandy laughed. At least Boris was consistent!

Sam Western stood in the doorway. 'I'll call by to settle the bill in a day or two,' he said, closing the door.

'It's usual to pay by cheque on collection of your pet . . .' Adam Hope started to say, but found he was talking to himself. The door had already closed.

'The cheek!' Mandy said, outraged.

Her father shrugged good-naturedly. 'There's one rule for Sam Western and one for everyone else. Oh, well. I know he'll settle sooner rather than later.'

Adam Hope drove away from Upper Welford Hall and headed for the high moors. The road twisted and turned as it became steeper. Mandy glimpsed the Beacon, which was a Celtic cross and a landmark for miles around. Welford lay spread out like a board-game in the valley below.

'Here you are, you two,' said Adam Hope, slowing down to a halt at the side of the road. Mandy and James got out. 'See you later!' They waved as the Land-rover turned into a stony track and headed for Lydia's farm.

'Race you!' Mandy flung herself on to her bike and set off at speed.

'You're on!' James hurtled after her.

Mandy bent forward over the handlebars as she sped down a long slope. Just as she was zooming past a drystone wall, James drew level with her. Mandy braked hard, then leaned against the wall, panting and laughing. 'I call that a draw!'

James took off his glasses and polished them on his sweater. He put them back on, then peered through the cleaned lenses. 'Hey! Is that who I think it is?'

Mandy looked across the fields. A doe and a well-grown fawn were nibbling bushes at the edge of the woods. She could just make out the fawn's blue ear tag. 'Honey-Mum and Sprite!' she gasped. 'Let's go over and say hello.'

They left their bikes and went slowly across the field on foot. Honey-Mum and Sprite lifted their heads, watching Mandy and James closely.

Just a bit nearer, Mandy thought. She took another step, then held out her hand. For a moment she thought the deer were going to turn away, then Sprite stepped forward on her long delicate legs.

She came right over and stopped in front of Mandy. Sprite's velvety nose quivered and her ears

swivelled. Mandy hardly dared move. Then Sprite reached her head forward.

Mandy felt a damp cold nose push at her hand. 'Oh, Sprite! You remember me,' she whispered delightedly.

'This is great,' murmured James. He fished in his shoulder-bag for his camera.

Mandy barely noticed what James was doing. 'You're so beautiful,' she breathed, stroking Sprite's graceful curved neck. She had a warm feeling in her chest. It was such a privilege to have a wild animal trust you.

Honey-Mum came forward and stood next to the fawn. She reached out her head and butted Mandy's arm. 'Do you want some fuss too?' Mandy murmured, stroking Honey-Mum's velvety ears.

In the background, Mandy could hear James clicking away with his camera. But she only had eyes for the deer. As James put his camera back in its case, he began stroking Honey-Mum and Sprite too.

Honey-Mum snuffled at James's hair. 'It feels funny!' he spluttered. 'All hot and tickly.'

Mandy laughed as James screwed up his face. Sprite began moving away, and Mandy gave her a final pat. 'Off you go, then.'

She and James stood and watched as Sprite and Honey-Mum wandered back to the bushes. Sprite's long legs carried her lightly through the grass. She stretched up her head and began nibbling at some oak leaves.

'Stay safe. And watch out for poachers,' Mandy whispered. She turned to James. 'Wasn't that wonderful?'

'The best,' he agreed as Sprite and Honey-Mum disappeared into the trees. 'Shall we go back to our bikes? I wouldn't mind riding round the edge of the wood.'

Mandy nodded. 'Fine by me.'

They jogged back across the field, then cycled down a track that led across the moors and came out near the woods. The sky was a clear bright blue against a row of yellow field maples.

'Hang on! Can we stop a minute?' James had spotted something he wanted to photograph. Mandy sat on her bike, watching James point his camera at a huge black crow sitting on a slab of limestone.

'Go it!' he said in triumph. 'I reckon that could be a winner!'

Mandy grinned. James said that every time he took a photo. They stopped twice more – once to photograph starlings massing around an oak tree, the other to snap a cheeky robin, picking grubs out of a drystone wall.

By now they had reached the road that circled the edge of Glisterdale forest. It was a warm day and Mandy was feeling hot. 'Let's stop for a drink by those trees,' she suggested, heading for a wide grass verge.

James was in front. Mandy saw him looking from side to side, still alert to anything that might be worth photographing. As he turned round to say something, a herd of deer broke cover and darted towards the road.

'Watch out!' she yelled.

James's head whipped back round. He braked hard and his bike slewed sideways in a shower of stones.

The deer leaped across the road only a metre or so in front of them. Their eyes were wide and panicked. More of them burst from the trees and dashed away across the open moor, scattering in all directions.

Mandy skidded to a halt.

'Phew! That was close,' James said shakily. 'Something must have scared them badly.'

'Yes!' Mandy's heart was beating fast. 'I didn't

see whether Sprite and Honey-Mum were with the herd. Did you?'

James shook his head and held up his hands. 'It happened so fast. But I think we'd have seen that blue ear tag.'

'Yes, of course,' Mandy agreed. She was grateful for James's cool logic, but she didn't know whether to feel worried or relieved.

Suddenly an explosion ripped through the air. High and sharp, it came rattling out of the trees. Gunfire! Mandy felt her stomach lurch. 'Poachers!' she said in a horrified whisper.

'Oh, no!' James's mouth dropped open.

Mandy's thoughts whirled. Visions of injured or dying deer crowded her head. There must be lots of other deer still in the forest, among them Sprite and Honey-Mum. What could they possibly do? Suddenly she knew. 'Come on!' She threw herself off her bike and dumped it on the grass.

'Shouldn't we tell someone?' James called.

But Mandy had made up her mind. 'In a minute. I've got to check that the deer are OK first.'

'Wait for me.' James's face was pale but determined. He threw his bike down next to Mandy's and entered the tangle of trees and bushes after her.

Mandy's heart was in her mouth as she crept forward and pushed the branches aside. The thick carpet of leaves rustled under her trainers. Loud shouts reached them. They could hear heavy boots crashing through the bracken. Suddenly, Mandy froze.

Through the trees, she could see a number of burly men grouped around a smart dark blue van. They all held guns. On the ground three deer lay unmoving in a pool of blood.

'Oh, no!' Mandy's stomach clenched in sadness and horror.

'Hurry up! Let's get these loaded,' one of the men ordered. He wore an expensive-looking dark green jacket and jeans tucked into wellingtons.

Mandy saw the deers' heads hanging limply as they were loaded into the van. Hot tears ran down her cheeks. This was so hateful, she could hardly bear it. Frantically, she searched for a fawn with a blue ear-tag. But Sprite wasn't among the fallen deer. Mandy squeezed her eyes tight shut in a moment of thanks. Sprite and Honey-Mum must have bolted deeper into the forest.

'Do you recognise any of the men?' James whispered in a shaky voice.

'No.' Mandy shook her head. She dashed away

her tears, a hard knot of anger building inside her. 'How dare they?' she hissed in outrage. 'They're shooting the deer in broad daylight!'

'They look pretty well organised, don't they? That bloke in the dark coat seems to be in charge,' said James. The man was talking to another man who had neat grey hair and a small moustache.

Mandy swallowed hard, trying to calm down enough to fix the men's faces in her memory.

'We can't help those deer now,' James said quietly. He pulled at Mandy's sleeve. 'Come on. We have to tell the police.'

James was right. Mandy took a final glance at the awful scene. The men had finished loading the deer. Mandy heard the slam of the van door closing. She noticed that the dark blue van had a deep scratch underneath the side window.

'Come on,' James urged again.

Mandy nodded, gulping back tears, and turned away to follow James. They edged back the way they had come, trying to make as little noise as possible. Ahead of Mandy, James had his head down, forging a way through the thick bushes.

Mandy spotted a flash of reddish brown through the trees off to one side. Oh, no. More deer were in danger! She turned, ready to go after the deer and shoo them away from the poachers. But there was no time.

Suddenly an explosion split the air behind her. Mandy jumped, her legs collapsing weakly under her.

'Run!' James yelled.

Mandy didn't need telling twice. She scrambled to her feet and hurtled through the trees. Brambles tangled in her hair and scratched her face, but she didn't stop.

More gunshots rang out, closer this time.

'Ow!' The noise resounded painfully in Mandy's ears. She stumbled and put her hands to her head.

James stopped and ran back to her. His eyes were wide and scared in his white face. Mandy saw his lips move, but she couldn't hear anything because of the loud ringing in her ears.

'Are – you – hurt?' James mouthed.

Mandy looked at him in confusion, feeling dazed and a bit sick. She shook her head to try and clear it. But her ears still rang.

James grabbed her arm and pulled her with him though the trees. Mandy stumbled along, trying to keep up, but her vision seemed blurred and her head throbbed and pounded as if someone was hammering at it from the inside.

Seven

On the ride home, Mandy clung grimly to her bike, moving her hands and feet mechanically. Her throat still ached with misery as she tried to put the horrible sight of the dead deer from her mind, but it seemed impossible.

James cycled along beside her, looking upset and worried. 'Are you still feeling dizzy? Do you want to stop?'

Mandy shook her head. His voice sounded all muffled. 'I just want to get home.'

It seemed to take for ever before they reached Welford. Mandy sighed with relief as they zoomed past the Fox and Goose crossroads and sped down the lane towards Animal Ark. James braked hard. He threw his bike down on the drive and helped Mandy dismount.

'Thanks. I'm feeling a bit better,' Mandy said. 'But my legs are wobbly.'

Emily Hope was in reception, speaking to Jean Knox. She took one look at Mandy and James, taking in their muddy jeans and strained faces. 'What's happened?' She came over and put her arm around Mandy.

'The poachers came back,' Mandy said, her voice sounding strange and hollow inside her head. Her eyes filled with tears. 'Oh, Mum. They shot some deer. It was awful. We saw them being loaded into a van.'

'We were leaving to get help when Mandy saw some more deer in danger,' said James.

'I was going to chase them away, but then there were some gunshots right near us,' Mandy said. 'It was so loud it hurt my ears.'

'Right.' Emily Hope looked grim as she took charge. She ushered them through to the kitchen where Mandy and James sank on to kitchen chairs. 'Don't move,' she ordered.

Mandy didn't think she could even if she wanted to. She felt utterly drained. James seemed to feel the same. He leaned forward in his chair, his hands hanging down between his knees.

Mandy watched as her mum picked up the phone and spoke to the police. 'Yes – in the woods, up near Upper Welford Hall. You will? Good. Thank you.' Mrs Hope looked serious as she replaced the phone. 'They're sending someone up there right away.'

'I hope they catch those monsters before they kill any more deer!' Mandy said in a choked voice. Then she glanced up at James. 'Do you think they shot the deer we saw when we were leaving?'

James shrugged miserably. 'Maybe. I don't know,' he murmured.

'I just hope they got away . . .' Mandy said, her voice trailing off.

Emily Hope came over and knelt on the floor by her daughter's chair. She smoothed Mandy's hair back from her face. 'It must have been really horrible for you and James.'

Mandy nodded: the pictures were fresh in her mind – the dark blue van, the hateful sound of the guns, the beautiful deer lying dead. 'What sort of people are they?' she burst out angrily. 'Haven't they got any feelings?'

Her mum patted her arm. 'I expect they are

more concerned with the money they'll make. It's hard to believe people can be so callous, isn't it? Luckily there are far more people in the world who care about animals.'

Mandy nodded. She felt the anger starting to fade. Her mum always seemed to know just the right thing to say.

'How do your ears feel now, love?'

'A bit strange,' Mandy admitted. 'I've still got ringing in my ears and everything sounds really weird. Am I going to be deaf now?' she asked worriedly. If this was how Echo felt, then no wonder she was timid and edgy all the time.

'Don't be silly!' Emily Hope laughed. 'The ringing will soon fade.'

'I feel a bit dizzy too,' Mandy said.

'Your balance is affected,' said her mum. 'That's normal with ear problems. It won't last long.' She looked at James and smiled. 'At least you seem to be in one piece.'

'I was in front of Mandy, so I was further away when we heard the gunshots,' said James.

'I almost fell over, but James grabbed me and pulled me on,' Mandy said.

'That was brave of you.' Emily Hope gave James a warm smile.

James blushed bright red. 'Anyone would have done it.'

'I'm not sure they would.' Mrs Hope pushed back a strand of her red hair. 'Now, I'd better wash these scratches on your face and hands, Mandy.'

Adam Hope came in to the kitchen as Emily Hope finished putting cream on Mandy's scratches. James was washing his muddy hands at the kitchen sink. 'Looks like someone's been in the wars,' said Mr Hope, looking concerned. 'What's been going on?'

Emily Hope lifted one eyebrow and gave Mandy and James a cool look. 'These two almost had a run in with the poachers. There was some shooting and Mandy was rather too close to the gunfire for comfort. The loud bangs hurt her ears.'

'What! You've been hurt?' Adam Hope looked alarmed.

Mandy had been staring glumly at the table. Now she spoke up hastily. 'It's OK, Dad. I'm fine . . .' She tailed off at the look on her dad's face.

'Well, thank goodness for that, Mandy!' her father said in an exasperated voice. 'Didn't you think of the danger?'

'Of course not,' Emily Hope answered for her daughter. 'She couldn't think of anything but the deer. Animals always come first with you, don't they, Mandy?'

Mandy bit her lip, but didn't reply. She was starting to feel guilty about worrying her mum and dad.

'I suppose you've informed the police?' Adam Hope said to his wife.

Emily Hope nodded. 'They're sending someone straight up there.'

'Oh, well. I suppose there's no real harm done,' Mr Hope said after a long pause. 'Although it looks like you two have had quite a fright.'

'We did,' Mandy and James agreed.

'So perhaps we'll say no more about this – this time,' Emily Hope decided in her clear sensible way. 'But will you promise me that you'll count to ten before rushing in next time?'

'I'll try,' Mandy promised.

'And pigs might fly,' James whispered, so that only she could hear.

Mandy dug him in the ribs. She knew that she'd been let off lightly.

'Yes, no more heroics, you two,' Adam Hope said firmly. 'Let the police take care of the poachers.'

'OK,' Mandy and James said together.

Mandy's father let out a long sigh. 'I don't know about anyone else, but I need a cup of tea.' He filled a kettle and put tea bags into mugs.

Mandy started to get up. The room seemed to tip and she swayed. It really was a strange sensation. 'Uh-oh!' She sat down again quickly.

Suddenly she thought of something. She turned to her mum and dad, her heart beating faster with excitement. 'Wait a minute! Could Echo have been deafened by gunshots? Julia said that Echo loves running in the woods by Upper Welford Hall.'

'It's a possibility,' said Mrs Hope cautiously. 'But I think any deafness from gunshots would only be temporary. Thanks, Adam.' She took the mug of tea her husband handed her.

'Oh.' Mandy frowned, unwilling to let go of her theory just yet. There was something else niggling at the back of her mind. What was it? Then she had it. 'Echo's got that sore lump on her head, hasn't she, Mum? You said you thought it was an older injury.'

Emily Hope listened closely and nodded. 'Yes. There seemed no obvious explanation for it, but it seemed to have healed over.'

Mandy warmed to her idea. 'If Echo was nearby when the guns went off, she'd have been terrified, wouldn't she? Maybe she bolted and hit her head on a tree or something. Could *that* make her deaf, do you think?'

'I suppose so,' agreed her mum, looking thoughtful. 'But it would be very unusual. It might be an idea to find out when Echo started behaving badly, and if Julia noticed the lump on her head around that time.'

'We could phone Julia. She might know something,' suggested James.

'Great idea,' Mandy said. 'I'll go and do it now.'

'I think you'll have a problem with that,' said Adam Hope.

'Why?' Mandy asked.

'Ever tried having a phone conversation with your ears ringing?' her dad teased gently.

'No problem,' Mandy said, undaunted. 'James can phone Julia. He can tell me what she says.'

'Fine by me,' said James.

'There's no stopping you, is there, Mandy Hope?' Emily Hope shook her head, smiling.

'Nope!' Mandy said. 'Come on, James. We'll use the phone in the hall.'

Julia Hampton answered the phone on the third ring.

'Hi, Julia,' said James. 'Mandy and I wanted to have a word with you about Echo. Is that OK?'

At Julia's answer, James gave Mandy a thumbs-up sign.

Mandy listened as James explained their idea about the gunshots and Echo hitting her head.

'Ask her if she heard anyone shooting up at the woods when she was taking Echo for a walk recently,' Mandy prompted.

James relayed Mandy's question. 'She says yes, she did,' he said, when Julia had finished speaking.

'When was that?' Mandy asked.

'Two weeks ago,' came the answer.

Mandy frowned. 'I think that ties in with what Mr Western said. He told us there had been signs of poachers around the area for a couple of weeks. Can you ask Julia if Echo's behaviour got worse in the last two weeks or so?'

James repeated to Julia what Mandy had said. He listened to Julia speaking for a few seconds, then he turned back to Mandy. 'Julia thinks we're on to something. She says Echo's behaviour has definitely got worse since she heard the gunshots!'

'Tell her to hang on a minute. I'll go and tell Mum and Dad,' Mandy said. She went into the kitchen to give them the news. 'Julia thinks we're right about Echo! Everything adds up. What should we do now?'

'Well, I'd still like to do some proper hearing tests on Echo before we jump to conclusions,' said Mrs Hope. 'Tell Julia she can bring Echo in tomorrow if her parents agree.'

'Sure thing!' Mandy hurried back to James.

James relayed Mandy's question. Julia checked with her parents, then told James that her mum and dad had agreed to bring Echo in to Animal Ark for more tests.

'OK. Bye. See you.' James put the phone down.

Mandy looked at him with eager shining eyes. 'Julia's going to be so relieved when she finds out that Echo's not just being difficult!'

'Maybe.' James didn't look convinced.

'What do you mean?' Mandy asked.

'Think about it,' James said logically. 'Julia's parents are fed up with Echo's behaviour. She's become such a problem that they want to find her a new home. So how do you think they are going to react when they find out Echo's deaf?'

Mandy's heart sank. She saw at once what James was getting at. She had thought that finding out what was wrong with Echo would solve everything. But it might actually stir up a whole lot of new problems for Julia and her parents.

Echo stayed on Mandy's mind all afternoon. And there were the poachers to worry about too. Had the police arrested the gang responsible yet? Were Honey-Mum and Sprite still in danger?

She felt restless and uneasy. The ringing in her ears didn't help her mood. Her mum had suggested she spend a few hours relaxing with a book.

'Poor you,' said Adam Hope, when he found her curled up on the red sofa in the sitting room. A log fire crackled in the hearth, making the room warm and cosy. Mandy's dad had one arm behind his back. 'How's the temporary invalid?' he asked, his eyes twinkling.

'Bored, bored, bored.' Mandy managed a glum smile. 'Mum said to leave my chores until later. I can't hear the TV properly, I've finished all my homework, and I don't fancy reading.'

'Not even these!' Adam whipped a hand from behind his back to reveal two glossy magazines.

Mandy's eyes widened at the sight of the front covers with their pictures of exotic monkeys and birds of paradise. 'Oh, wow! Brilliant! These are great.'

Adam Hope grinned. 'I thought we could do with some new reading matter for the waiting room. The old magazines are falling to bits, so I took a quick trip to McFarlane's.'

Mandy grinned at her dad. He didn't fool her one bit – he had bought them to cheer her up. She threw her arms round him and gave him a hug. 'Thanks, Dad!'

'No problem, love. I'll see you later. I'm on duty in the surgery now.' He pulled a face. 'Mrs

Ponsonby is coming in. Pandora is due for a booster injection.'

'Good luck then!' Mandy chuckled. Mrs Ponsonby was the bossiest woman in the village, but she doted on her spoilt Pekingese, Pandora, and her lively mongrel puppy, Toby.

Mandy settled back on the sofa with the magazines. She was so engrossed that the rest of the afternoon passed quickly. She checked the clock and, finding it was almost time for supper, she leaped to her feet.

'Hey!' She stopped dead. The ringing had stopped and she no longer felt dizzy.

She dashed off to find her mum and dad and tell them the news. But a shadow passed over her good mood as she thought about Echo's tests the next day. Poor Echo – it looked like her problem wasn't going to be so easily resolved.

Eight

First thing the following morning, Mandy pulled on her jumper as she flew down the stairs and almost collided with her mum as she came out of the kitchen.

'Hey! Where's the fire?' Emily Hope teased.

'Sorry, Mum!' Mandy apologised. 'But I can't stop thinking about what happened in the woods yesterday. Could you phone the police, please?'

Mrs Hope nodded. 'I'll do it right away. I'm as anxious as you are to know if those men have been caught.'

She went into the hall. Mandy waited impatiently as she heard her mum talking to the police.

When Mrs Hope came back into the kitchen, Mandy searched her face eagerly. 'What did they say?' she asked. 'Did they arrest the poachers?'

Emily Hope shook her head. 'I'm afraid not, love. They sent someone up there straight after I phoned yesterday. They found plenty of evidence of poaching, but there was no sign of anyone.'

Mandy's spirits sank. This was awful. Somehow she didn't think that the poachers had finished up at Glisterdale Forest. They could come back at any time, which meant that Honey-Mum's and Sprite's lives were still at risk.

'Try not to think about the poachers, love,' Mrs Hope went on gently. 'Worrying never solves anything.'

'I know,' Mandy replied, thinking that her mum was right, but that it was easier said than done.

Just then Adam Hope came in from the back garden. He went to the sink to wash his hands. 'I'll never know how we manage to fill so many rubbish bags. I must have put out at least a hundred of them for collection.'

'Oh, sure!' Mandy laughed. And to think her dad was always teasing her for exaggerating! 'Sick animals can't help using up lots of bedding and stuff, can they?' she said.

'No. It's all part of the job,' Mr Hope agreed cheerfully, as he dried his hands. 'And I used to think being a vet was glamorous!'

Mandy pulled a face. 'It is!' she said firmly. 'It's the best job in the world!'

'Now, how did I know that you'd say that?' Mr Hope grinned as he filled the kettle and switched it on. 'I'm ready for some tea and toast. Anyone want to join me?'

Mandy was thoughtful as she ate her toast. Only a few days left now before term started. She loved school and was looking forward to catching up with friends she hadn't seen over the holidays. After they finished eating, Mandy helped clear away the dishes, then she went to do her chores. It wasn't very exciting to clean out cages and mop floors, but she knew it was an important part of animal care.

Just as she was putting the cleaning things back in their cupboard, Adam Hope popped his head round the door. 'Julia and her parents are here,' he told her.

'Brilliant timing! Thanks, Dad.' Mandy followed him through into the waiting room.

She found Julia and her parents sitting anxiously in a row. 'Hi, Julia. Hi, Mr and Mrs Hampton,' Mandy said.

'Hello, Mandy,' said Mrs Hampton with a rather strained smile.

'How's Echo been?' Mandy asked Julia.

'About the same,' said Julia. 'We've been keeping her in, except for short runs in the back garden. I really miss taking her out for walks.'

'Your mum's just taken Echo to be examined,' Mr Hampton said to Mandy. 'We were really shocked when Julia told us about the gunshots and how they could have affected Echo.'

'It's awful, isn't it?' Mandy agreed sadly. 'It looks like poor Echo's been really unlucky.'

Julia nodded miserably, close to tears. 'It's just not fair! Echo passed all her hearing tests when she was little, but now she might have been made deaf anyway!' She looked down and began twisting her hands in her lap.

Mr Hampton put a hand on his daughter's shoulder. 'Echo's getting the best treatment now, love. We'll soon know how she is,' he said gently.

'That's right. I expect Mum's doing the tests now,' Mandy said reassuringly.

Julia's head came up. 'Will they hurt her?' she asked anxiously.

'Oh, no.' Mandy reassured the worried girl. 'Mum will look inside her ears to check for any physical damage first. Then she'll go through a special routine. Basically, she'll stand behind Echo and make different noises. She marks the findings on a chart and the results will show Echo's level of hearing.'

'It doesn't sound too frightening,' Julia said, seeming to relax a bit, but her friendly face still looked strained. Mandy guessed Julia had spent a sleepless night worrying about her pet.

'Thanks for explaining that, Mandy,' said Mrs Hampton.

'That's all right,' Mandy said, wishing there was more she could do.

Just then two more owners and their pets came into the waiting room. As the reception became busier and other patients arrived, Mandy went to help Jean Knox.

'Thanks, Mandy,' said the receptionist, looking up from her appointment book.

Adam Hope dealt with each patient in turn. He called to Mandy to ask for her help and she gave him a hand to keep a Jack Russell pup calm while he dressed the pup's cut paw.

'Thanks, love,' said Mandy's dad when the Jack Russell and his owner had left. 'Why don't you go back and sit with Julia now?'

'OK.' But Mandy had hardly sat down when her mum appeared at the door of the treatment room.

'Would you like to come in now?' Emily Hope called out.

Mandy followed Julia and her parents inside. Echo didn't look round when everyone trooped in. She stood gazing at the floor, her head drooping slightly.

Julia went straight across to her dog and gave her a hug. Echo jumped at first, but seemed to relax when she recognised her owner's smell and touch.

'How is she?' Julia asked worriedly, stroking Echo.

'It's as we thought, I'm afraid,' said Mrs Hope. 'Echo has gone deaf. We'll probably never be sure what happened to her. But I think Echo was running in the woods when someone fired a gun very close by. It would have hurt her ears and probably confused and terrified her. My guess is that she panicked and ran into a tree or maybe a rock. That would explain the lump on her head.'

'Deaf? You see, Dad! Mum! Echo can't help her bad behaviour.' Julia leaped to her dog's defence at once. 'Poor Echo! She's had a horrible shock. It's no wonder she's so frightened and confused.'

'What an awful thing to happen.' Mrs Hampton shook her head sadly. She reached out and stroked Echo. 'She used to be such a lovely-natured dog.'

'She still is!' Mandy burst out, going round to stand in front of Echo. She cupped the dog's face in her hands like she had seen Elise do to Maisy. 'You're gorgeous, aren't you?'

Julia watched closely as Echo wagged her tail and licked Mandy's chin. 'She didn't jump at all when you touched her just now,' she said with surprise.

'That's because I made sure she could see me first. Once she knew I was there and what I was doing, she felt OK,' Mandy explained. 'You try it.'

Julia copied Mandy's actions. This time Echo stood placidly while Julia petted her. Julia looked pleased. 'Good girl, Echo. Thanks, Mandy.'

Emily Hope turned to Julia's parents. 'Now that we know what Echo's problem is, we can discuss your options.'

'Options?' Julia's dad repeated. 'Well, I can't help feeling that we've got an even bigger problem now.'

'What do you mean?' Julia rounded on her dad, her smile fading.

'Think about it, love. This isn't what we expected at all when we bought the dog. How's Echo going to lead a normal life? For a start, she needs loads of exercise, but you can't let her run free any more.'

'Why not?' Julia protested, putting her arm protectively round Echo's neck.

'Because she can't hear you calling her back. I expect that's why she's run away twice already,' Julia's mum added. She looked towards Emily Hope as if for confirmation.

Mrs Hope nodded gravely. 'That's probably true,' she said.

'Oh.' Julia bit her lip. She seemed to be starting to see her mum and dad's point of view.

Mr Hampton spoke up. 'And what about the effect this has on Echo's temperament? I can see why she's been so nervous recently, but even though we know the reason it doesn't mean we can do anything about it. We're going to have to start all over again with her training.'

'I won't deny that it will take a lot of time and patience,' agreed Emily Hope.

Julia's eyes filled with tears. 'But I want to help Echo. I just don't know where to start.'

Mandy stroked Echo's smooth neck. Echo whined softly, then turned and licked her hand. 'Elise Knight felt like that at first,' Mandy said. She explained that Elise was a local writer and that Maisy was her deaf Dalmatian. 'Now Elise says she wouldn't be without Maisy. They get on brilliantly and you'd never know that Maisy couldn't hear,' she finished.

'But if Elise is a writer, she probably works from home,' Julia's dad pointed out. 'That means she can give her dog all the time she needs. Julia will be back at school in a few days.'

Julia turned to her parents eagerly. 'That doesn't matter! I'll take Echo out early every morning. And I'll have evenings and weekends too. I know I can cope, especially if you'll both help me . . .'

Julia's mum shook her head slowly. 'Julia, love,' she said reasonably, 'I really think this is beyond us. We have to face facts.'

Julia looked at each of her parents in turn. 'So what are you saying? That we aren't even going to try?'

Mandy couldn't stay silent. 'But there's loads you can do for Echo! There are special dog whistles. And you can train dogs to respond to hand signals. James and I could help Julia, just like we helped Elise with Maisy . . .'

'That's enough, Mandy,' her mum said firmly. 'I know you want to help. But let's keep the suggestions back until everyone's thought about this.'

Mandy knew her mum was right. But was there nothing anyone could say to persuade the Hamptons to keep Echo? She looked desperately at Julia. Surely she wanted to do everything possible for Echo?

Julia seemed to be finding the whole thing too much to bear. She gave a little sound of distress and buried her head in Echo's neck. 'There has to be a way, Echo. I won't give up,' she murmured tearfully.

Mrs Hampton patted her daughter's shoulder. 'I'm sorry, love. But I really think it would be better if we ask the Hopes if they can find a new home for Echo as soon as possible,' she said gently.

Emily Hope waited for a moment, then she nodded. 'I'll do my best, if that's what you want.'

'It isn't what we want, but I can't see any other way,' said Mr Hampton heavily.

'I understand,' said Mrs Hope. 'It's a difficult situation for you all.'

'Thank you so much for everything you've done for Echo,' Mrs Hampton added. She gave Echo a stroke. 'Poor girl,' she said softly.

Mandy's heart sank. Echo was so lovely. Surely she deserved a chance to stay with her owners? She cast a pleading look at her mother. 'Isn't there some other way . . .'

Emily Hope held up her hand. 'Hang on, Mandy. This has to be Julia's and her parents' decision.'

Julia raised a tear-stained face. 'Does . . . does Echo have to stay here?' she asked.

'No. We'll take her home,' Julia's dad said kindly. 'But only until a new owner can be found.'

Mandy had a lump in her throat as she watched Julia stand in front of Echo and look into her eyes. Then she took hold of the lead and tugged it gently. 'Come on, girl,' said Julia, tapping Echo on her shoulder. Echo's head came up, her tail wagged, and she trotted out obediently.

'Julia's a natural,' Mandy thought. She was sure that with a little help, Julia would be able to re-train Echo. But it looked as if she wasn't going to get the chance.

'Time for a break,' announced Emily Hope, when Julia and Echo had gone. 'And that's an order!'

Mandy trudged glumly through to the kitchen after her mum. She sat in a kitchen chair and propped her chin on her hand while Emily Hope made them both hot chocolate and piled biscuits on a plate.

'Cheer up, love,' she said. 'If you're going to be a vet, you'll need to learn that there's a point where you have to hang back and not get involved.'

'I know,' Mandy said. 'But sometimes it's really hard.' She sipped her chocolate. 'You know, Mum, Glisterdale Forest is lovely, but it seems to bring nothing but bad luck at the moment.'

'How do you mean?' asked Mrs Hope.

'Well,' Mandy replied. 'First there's poor Echo, then there's the poachers who haven't been caught yet. They could even be killing more deer right now.' She let out a long sigh. 'I'd really like something good to happen for a change!'

Nine

Mandy was in the recovery room when James arrived the following day. Her mum had been keeping an eye on Pippin, an old rabbit who had reacted badly to the anaesthetic. Mandy had popped in to check on him. 'How is he?' she asked.

'Pippin's coming round now. He'll be fine,' said Mrs Hope.

'That's good,' Mandy said, pushing open the door and going into the surgery. She saw James through the window. 'James's here, Mum! I'll see you later.'

'OK. Bye,' Emily Hope called after her.

James had brought Blackie with him and he had

binoculars and a camera slung over his shoulder. Mandy went outside to meet them. 'Hi, James. Hi, Blackie.' The Labrador gave a friendly woof and wagged his tail as Mandy patted his head.

'I thought we could take Blackie up to the dales for a walk,' James suggested. 'We still need to take some photos for the competition. I've only got those ones of . . . er . . . so far,' he faltered.

'Of what?' Mandy asked, puzzled.

'Nothing. Doesn't matter,' said James quickly.

Mandy shrugged. A walk was fine by her. It might take her mind off poor Echo. 'OK,' she said. 'But I don't think we'll see much wildlife if we have Blackie with us!'

James pretended to be hurt. 'I can always call him to heel. He's doing really well at dog training classes. Watch this. He's been learning to lie down on command.'

Mandy watched as James gave a gentle tug on the lead. 'Down,' he said firmly.

Blackie's ears pricked up. He gave a short bark, then jumped up and put his paws on James's chest.

'Oh, very impressive!' Mandy laughed as Blackie licked James's chin.

'Get off, Blackie!' James blushed and wiped his chin. 'OK, so he's still got some learning to do.'

'You can say that again! Never mind. Blackie's lovely just the way he is.' Mandy stroked the Labrador's soft ears. 'You wait here. I'll just pop back into the house and change into my boots.'

Adam Hope was in the kitchen. His white vet's coat was covered in muddy marks. 'Wet sheepdog with a gum infection – and a bad temper,' he explained with a grin as he stripped off the soiled coat.

Mandy reached into a cupboard for her

wellingtons. 'Are its teeth OK now?' she asked.

Her dad nodded. 'They will be once the antibiotic takes effect. But I don't know if this coat will recover!' Mandy laughed. Mr Hope tipped some washing powder into the slot, opened the door and bundled the coat in. He switched the machine on and looked towards the open back door where James waited with Blackie. 'Where are you two – or should I say three – off to?'

'We're taking Blackie for a walk to get some more photos,' Mandy told him. She had pulled on her boots and was zipping up her anorak.

'Good luck, then. See you later!' Adam Hope went out to get a clean white coat.

'Bye, Dad.'

'Bye, Mr Hope,' called James.

They went along the lane, where the hawthorn bushes were heavy with dark red berries. Mandy suggested they cut across the fields. It had rained hard in the night and the stubble was sodden underfoot.

'Heel,' James said hopefully as Blackie pulled at his lead. But Blackie took no notice. His nose was twitching at all the delicious scents.

Mandy soon felt her head beginning to clear as they climbed higher in the fresh autumn air.

'I'll let Blackie off now. We're miles from the road,' said James, unclipping the lead. Blackie trotted off to sniff out tracks in the grass.

Mandy and James splashed through the puddles. They kept an eye open for anything worth photographing. Birds circled high overhead, tiny black dots against the grey sky.

Mandy borrowed James's binoculars. 'Look! There's a squirrel in that tree!' She passed them over to James.

James peered at the squirrel. 'Nice. But it's a bit far away for a good photo.'

'What about those rabbits on top of that hill?' Mandy said.

Suddenly Blackie barked and shot forward. He'd seen the rabbits too. The Labrador laid back his ears and bounded across the field.

'Uh-oh!' Mandy said. She knew that Blackie had a one-track mind once he'd glimpsed the white bobtail of a rabbit.

'We'd better go after him!' James gasped.

Mandy and James stumbled up the long steep slope, the mud sticking to their wellies. By the time she reached the crest of the hill, Mandy was breathing hard. She looked out over the wide sweep of the dales. 'He's nowhere in sight,' she said.

James paused at her side. 'He could be anywhere.' He lifted the binoculars and scanned the slabs of limestone rock and open moorland that stretched into the distance.

Then Mandy glimpsed a dark shape between some trees in the valley bottom. 'He's down there! Come on,' she said, setting off again.

It was easier running downhill, but the wet grass was slippery. Mandy and James skidded to a halt in front of some birch trees just as Blackie came lolloping towards them. His tongue was hanging out and his breath steamed as he gave them a doggy grin.

'Where have you been?' James scolded. He made a grab for Blackie's collar, but it was too late. The Labrador turned tail and shot off through the trees.

Mandy groaned. 'Here we go again!'

'I'll never get any photos at this rate!' James complained.

Mandy thought it best not to remind him that it had been his idea to bring Blackie. They plunged into the trees after the black Labrador. It soon became even more soggy underfoot. Mandy saw water glinting through the birches. 'What's that splashing noise?' she began.

James rolled his eyes. 'Oh, no,' he groaned. 'He wouldn't . . .'

They emerged into a small clearing. The ground sloped down on all sides and a large pool of rainwater had gathered in the bottom. Blackie was rolling over and over in the leafy mud at the edge of the water. He seemed to be thoroughly enjoying himself.

'Blackie, stop that! Come here!' James yelled.

The Labrador stood up. His nose was wet and his thick black fur stuck up in muddy spikes. Mandy couldn't help laughing.

'Oh, that's just great. Mum will go mad!' James's face was red and annoyed. 'I'll have to bath him when we get home.'

'Don't worry. I'll help,' Mandy promised. 'We can clean him up at Animal Ark, if you like.'

James brightened. 'Thanks.' Then he began to laugh too. 'Blackie, you idiot! Look at the state of you!'

'There might not be a Dalmatian in the dales any more,' Mandy said. But there's definitely a mutt in the mud!'

Blackie blinked happily at them, his eyelashes spiky as well. His tail wagged merrily.

Suddenly, Mandy stiffened. On the far side of

the glade, a group of deer were stepping out of the trees. They were fallow deer – mostly does and fawns, but there was a buck with them too.

'Don't make any sudden movements,' Mandy whispered urgently.

'What?' James turned his head very slowly and drew in his breath. 'Oh wow! I must get my camera.'

The deer bent their slender copper-coloured necks and began drinking. The buck kept watch. His proud head was crowned with impressive spreading antlers. Mandy looked through James's binoculars. 'He's starting to shed the velvet on his antlers, can you see?' she asked.

'Yes. Isn't it brilliant?' James whispered back as he clicked away excitedly.

Mandy caught hold of Blackie's collar and patted his wet head. Blackie was still panting hard and seemed content to lay down, so Mandy was able to study the buck in peace. She knew that the velvet was a special sort of skin that covered the antlers until they were fully grown. 'It's amazing that the bucks grow a completely new set of antlers every year, isn't it?' she said. 'And every year they get more points on the antlers' branches. You can tell their age by how many there are.' She counted the points. 'This one's six years old.'

'Mmm.' James was engrossed in peering through the viewfinder. After a couple of minutes, the camera whirred loudly as it rewound the film. 'That's it! I've used up all the film.'

Just in time, Mandy thought. The deer were looking over at them nervously. Suddenly the buck gave a coughing bark and they all melted back into the trees.

'That was brilliant!' James enthused.

'Success at last! And it's all down to Blackie finding this pool for us,' Mandy said. She would have given Blackie a hug if he hadn't been so muddy.

James stowed his camera away in its case. 'I suppose we ought to make our way back to Animal Ark. It's going to take ages to get Blackie cleaned up.'

'Fine by me,' Mandy agreed. 'Shall we go up to the road and go home the easy way?'

'Good idea,' said James. 'That way, Blackie's not likely to want to go chasing rabbits again.'

'Or take another mud bath!' Mandy added with a chuckle. 'Although I don't think he could get any messier if he tried!'

They climbed up the slope and out of the clearing, As they made their way over the rough moorland on their way up to the road, a thin rain began to fall. Mandy shivered as grey clouds drifted in lower over the rolling hills, glad that they were going home. She thought longingly of the cosy kitchen and mugs of hot chocolate.

As they reached the road, James clipped on Blackie's lead and they started walking back towards Welford. Just then a dark blue van came speeding along the road towards them. It zoomed by and disappeared around a bend. Mandy felt a clutching sensation in her chest. It was the poachers' van!

'James! Did you see that?' she gasped.

James stood stock still. He nodded. 'It was heading for the woods!'

'You know what that means. More deer will be killed!' Mandy said furiously. Before she could think better of it, she turned and sprinted after the van. 'Come on,' she called over her shoulder. 'We have to do something!'

James ran after Mandy, Blackie loping along at his side.

Mandy's long legs carried her swiftly up the roads to the woods. She saw a car park ahead and dashed into it. She panted to a halt, looking left and right. No sign of the blue van. Then she spotted a forestry track, leading deeper into the trees. 'Over here!' she called to James. 'That track must be how they get to the deer!' She began heading after them.

James caught up with her. 'Hang on a minute. What's the plan?'

'I'll try and think of a way to distract the poachers,' Mandy puffed, thinking fast. 'Or maybe I can find the deer and chase them away out of danger. You run for help. Upper Welford Hall's on the other side of the forest. It'll be quicker to go there than run all the way back to the village!'

'I'm not leaving you on your own,' James protested.

Mandy hadn't got time to argue. 'I'll be OK. Just go!'

James seemed torn. Mandy thought he was going to insist on staying. Then he made up his mind. He thrust Blackie's lead into her hands. 'All right. I'll be as quick as I can. But I'm leaving Blackie with you!'

Mandy watched James speed away down the track. Her heart was thudding painfully. She set off again, praying that Blackie would behave himself for once. She felt desperate as she crashed through the trees. She just knew that she had to do anything possible to save even one more deer from being killed.

Branches whipped past her face as she kept alert for any movement. Suddenly she glimpsed the honey-gold coats of a group of young does. She took a deep breath and ran straight at the deer. 'Come on, Blackie!' she urged.

Luckily the Labrador seemed to understand what she wanted. He leaped forward, matching her pace.

Mandy waved her arms and shouted. 'Run away. Shoo! Go on. Run!'

From the corner of her eye, she glimpsed a part of the fence that ringed the woods. If she could just get the deer to jump it, they would be safe on the open moor. The startled does had retreated further back into the trees, but they paused a few metres away. Looking back at Mandy, they blinked curiously.

'Oh, no,' she groaned. Normally she would have been delighted that the does seemed interested in her. She would have loved to gain their trust. But now she had to try to scare them for their own good.

She ran towards them again, her arms waving like windmills. 'Go on! What are you waiting for?' she shouted desperately. 'Run!'

It was no use. The deer didn't move. Mandy almost sobbed with frustration. They would be easy targets if they stayed here.

Then Blackie surged forward again, almost pulling the lead from her hand. He gave a series of loud barks. The doe at the head of the group made a sharp little coughing noise. She stamped her feet and raised her tail to show the white fur underneath.

'That's it, Blackie. Good boy! Keep barking!' Mandy encouraged.

She watched as the doe warned the others of danger. Then they all turned tail and hurtled towards the fence.

'Yes!' Mandy called out in triumph. She let out a long sigh, watching as they reached the fence and each one of them sailed over it to the open moor. This time she could be certain that the deer were safe.

Mandy fell to her knees and hugged Blackie – mud and all. 'Good boy!' she praised him again. 'We did it. We saved the deer!'

Blackie whined and licked her face.

As Mandy rose to her feet, a cold breeze swept damp autumn mist all round her and she felt a surge of satisfaction. The mist would make it even harder for the poachers to follow the deer.

Suddenly a large dark shape came looming out of the trees. The poachers' van! There was no time to run. It came roaring down the track and screeched to a halt right in front of her.

Ten

Mandy's mouth dried. Her legs felt as if they had turned to jelly.

The van doors opened and three tough-looking men got out. Mandy recognised two of them from the other day, including the one wearing the dark jacket who seemed to be in charge.

Blackie growled menacingly. 'Down, boy,' she said, grabbing his collar to stop him leaping towards the van. Mandy swallowed hard, shaking with fright. But her chin came up as she glared defiantly at the men. She gave a small tug on Blackie's lead, urging him to walk forward with her. As she walked past the men, they stood and watched her.

Despite her fear, Mandy had a warm feeling inside her, because she knew that she had beaten them. Whatever the men did now, they couldn't harm the deer she had chased away.

The poachers seemed unsure what to do about her. Then one of them started to come towards her. Blackie's hackles rose. He growled warningly and the man hesitated.

'The police are on their way!' Mandy burst out, praying that it was true. James should have reached Upper Welford Hall by now.

She saw the men glance uneasily at each other.

Then the leader allowed his frown to relax a fraction. 'She's bluffing,' he said. 'Let's get on with it.'

Mandy's confidence slipped away. They were still going to look for deer! There seemed nothing else she could do. She had scared away one small group of deer, but there would be others nearby. And Honey-Mum and Sprite might be with them.

The men were opening the van and reaching for their guns. Blackie surged forward again, barking loudly and pulling against his collar. Mandy almost lost her balance as she tried to hang on to him.

'What about the dog?' One of the men eyed Blackie warily.

'I'll deal with it,' said the leader. He stood there, the shiny steel barrel of his shotgun gleaming menacingly. The polished wooden butt rested under his arm. He took a step towards Mandy and began to raise the gun.

'Oh, no! No!' Mandy's blood ran cold. She curved an arm protectively around Blackie's thick neck and squeezed her eyes shut.

There was a screech of brakes. Mandy's eyes flew open as three vehicles appeared through the trees, two police vans and Sam Western's Land-rover. Mandy heard doors slam, then loud voices rang out.

'Put down the guns! You're all under arrest!'

Mandy recognised the voice of Sergeant Wilkins, the wildlife officer from the police headquarters at Walton. She saw that policemen were piling out of the vans. They surrounded the poachers and the men laid their guns down without protest.

It was all over. Mandy's legs gave way. She sank down beside Blackie and hugged him close. His gritty wet fur felt wonderful against her cheek.

James scrambled out of Mr Western's Land-rover and came tearing over. His eyes looked huge and scared behind his glasses. 'Are you OK?' he asked anxiously. 'I . . . I saw that man aim his gun . . .'

Mandy looked up and smiled weakly. She blinked back tears. 'We're both fine. Blackie was a brilliant guard dog.'

James bent down and gave his pet a hug. 'Well done, boy!'

'You must have run like mad to have got back so soon,' Mandy said.

'Not really. I got winded before I was halfway to Upper Welford Hall,' James admitted. 'I was trying to catch my breath, when Sam Western came along in his Land-rover. As soon as I told him what was going on, he called the police on his mobile.'

Mandy beamed at him. 'Well, I think you did great, James Hunter!'

James blushed, but looked delighted. 'What about you? Did you manage to chase the deer away?'

'Oh, yes,' Mandy said with deep satisfaction. 'A whole lot of them jumped the fence. You, me, and Blackie did it together. We saved the deer!'

James grinned from ear to ear. 'That's great,' he said.

'We haven't done anything!' one of the poachers was protesting angrily. 'You can check the guns. They haven't been fired.'

'Maybe not today,' James muttered under his breath.

'You can't arrest us without evidence!' said the leader.

Mandy and James looked at each other in dismay. Surely the men weren't going to be allowed to get away?

But Sam Western was marching over to the poachers' van. He opened the back door and peered inside. 'Have a look at this, sergeant,' he called out with grim satisfaction. 'I think you'll find all the evidence you'll need right here!'

Two policemen went over the van.

'Just as well they didn't scrub it out,' said Sam Western. 'It should be no problem to check for traces of deer.'

'Oh, I've no doubt about what we'll find,' Sergeant Wilkins agreed.

'I need to call my solicitor,' the leader of the poachers said coolly. The other men didn't say anything. They seemed to realise that it was useless to argue as the police led them away.

Sergeant Wilkins came over to Mandy. 'Hello there,' he said. 'Fighting on the side of the animals again, eh? Well done, you two. We've been after this gang for some time. You can be sure that they'll be out of action for quite a while!'

'Good!' Mandy said with feeling. 'That means no more deer will be killed.'

Sergeant Wilkins nodded. 'Right. It's a good thing the deer had you and James looking out for them.'

'They're all safe now. That's the main thing,' Mandy said. She was cold, muddy and she still felt a bit shaky, but she was utterly satisfied with how things had turned out.

Sam Western appeared at her shoulder. 'You look frozen, young lady,' he said in his curt way. 'There's a blanket in the Land-rover. Come on. Get in and

I'll give you and your friend a lift home.'

'Thanks, Mr Western. A lift would be great.' Mandy pushed a strand of damp blonde hair out of her face.

'Think nothing of it,' came the brusque reply. 'Besides, I'd like a word or two with your mum and dad.'

Mandy groaned inwardly as she climbed into the Land-rover. She was going to have some more explaining to do, especially as her parents had told her not to go back into the forest.

'You'd better put your dog in the back,' Sam Western said to James.

'Thanks.' James put the Labrador in the back behind the dog screen, then he got in and sat beside Mandy. He gave her a shaky smile. 'Whatever you do, don't mention the forbidden word when we get back!'

'What word?' Mandy asked.

'B-A-T-H.' James spelled it out.

Mandy grinned. Blackie might adore rolling in smelly mud, but he'd run a mile if he heard the word bath!

Back at Animal Ark, Mandy was soon warming herself in front of the fire in the sitting room, her hands cupped round a hot drink. She was in deep trouble.

'Will you never learn not to go charging into dangerous situations?' Emily Hope's voice rang with exasperation and concern.

'I'm with your mum on this one,' Adam Hope agreed. 'Whatever possessed you, Mandy? And after what happened the other day!'

'You would have done the same! I know you would!' Mandy protested. 'I had to save the deer from getting shot. If I hadn't chased them away, lots more of them would be dead by now.'

'Maybe Honey-Mum and Sprite with them,' James put in, trying to help.

'That's probably true,' admitted Mr Hope. 'But even so . . .'

'I have to agree with Mandy on this.' Unexpectedly, Sam Western spoke up. 'I'm grateful she acted as she did. By saving those deer, she also saved me a lot of money.'

James glanced at Mandy. 'Can you believe it? He's on our side for once!' he murmured. 'But only because there's money involved.'

Mandy raised her eyebrows.

Sam Western checked his wristwatch. 'I'll have to be getting back now. I need to go over to Walton to make a statement to the police.'

'Thanks for bringing Mandy and James back,' said Emily Hope. She went out to see Sam Western to the door.

Mandy looked at her dad. 'Sorry,' she said. 'I didn't mean to worry you and Mum.'

'You never do,' Adam Hope said with a sigh. 'What about the promise you made to keep out of those woods?'

'I know,' Mandy replied miserably. What could she say? She had been let off lightly last time because her ears had been hurt. This time her parents seemed really annoyed, and she didn't blame them.

Emily Hope had returned. She shook her head slowly, but she looked less angry. 'You'll turn us grey with worry. What are we going to do with you?' she said.

'Ground me for a week?' Mandy suggested.

'Sounds good to me,' her dad said. 'Emily?'

'And double chores?' said Emily Hope, a smile pulling at the corners of her mouth.

'Oh.' Mandy's face fell.

'I think being grounded for a week will do,' Adam Hope decided, winking at his wife.

'Thanks, Mum, Dad,' Mandy said, giving them

both a hug. 'Now that the deer are safe, I promise not to get into any more trouble!'

Adam Hope stroked his beard. 'Until the next time.'

'Hot soup and toast everyone?' asked Emily Hope.

'Yes, please!' Mandy and James said together.

'And then James and I have one muddy dog to bath!' Mandy said. 'Oh, no. I went and said it!'

She clapped both hands over her mouth. Too late. Blackie's ears had pricked up. He whined and crouched down so that his stomach brushed the floor. Then he crept towards the kitchen table.

Mandy looked at Blackie, who was trying to hide his stocky body behind the table leg. A laugh spilled out of her. 'Oh, Blackie, you're priceless! What are we going to do with you?'

'Bribery always works!' said James.

After tucking into their soup and toast, Mandy and James used dog biscuits to persuade Blackie into the veterinary residential unit. Blackie stood in the big sink at the back, which was used for washing animals.

Mandy began hosing Blackie with warm water. James squirted dog shampoo into his hand, then worked it into Blackie's thick coat. 'Being grounded isn't so bad. Blackie and I can always come over to see you,' he said.

Mandy nodded. 'And it's a small price to pay for knowing that Honey-Mum and Sprite are safe!'

Blackie seemed resigned to his ordeal. He sat quietly while he was soaped and rinsed. Then Mandy and James rubbed him briskly with a towel.

'This is the tricky bit,' puffed James, as he and Mandy struggled to lift Blackie out. Blackie kept still as they put him on to the floor. 'Good boy,' James praised him.

'Watch he doesn't shake himself now,' Mandy warned as she reached for the hair dryer. She switched it on and ruffled warm air through Blackie's wet coat.

James picked up a brush and Blackie was soon gleaming like polished coal.

'Ah! His fur's all fluffy, just like when he was a pup!' said James.

They both laughed. Blackie's ears were flat against his head. He gave them a disgusted look, but he wagged his tail.

Mandy gave him a cuddle. 'You look very smart!'

'Smart and brave!' James added proudly, ruffling Blackie's ears.

Seeing James with Blackie reminded Mandy of Echo and Julia. She'd hardly had time to think about them lately, with all the excitement of the poachers. But now things had calmed down she began worrying again about the deaf Dalmatian.

'I wonder if I should phone Julia?' she said. 'I bet she's feeling terrible.'

James nodded. 'Poor thing. It's a shame Echo's having to be re-homed, isn't it? I couldn't imagine not having Blackie.'

'No. Me neither,' Mandy agreed.

'Do you think there's any way the Hamptons will change their minds about keeping Echo?' asked James.

Mandy shook her head. 'They seemed pretty convinced that they couldn't cope with the extra training.'

James looked thoughtful. 'What we need is some way of showing Julia and her parents that re-training Echo isn't beyond them.'

A light seemed to come on in Mandy's head. 'Did anyone ever tell you you're brilliant, James Hunter?'

'All the time,' James joked.

'No, listen,' Mandy said eagerly. 'We could invite Julia and her parents to come to Animal Ark.

Then we can ask Elise to bring Maisy along as well.'

James looked impressed. 'So that they just happen to be here when the Hamptons arrive with Echo, you mean?'

'Yes,' Mandy said. 'If Julia's parents see how well Elise gets along with Maisy, they might change their minds about re-homing Echo.'

'Great idea. I'm glad I thought of it,' said James with a cheeky grin. 'It just might work.'

'Right.' Mandy couldn't wait to put their plan into action. 'As soon as we finish tidying up, I'll go and make the phone calls.'

Eleven

Elise arrived with Maisy on Thursday afternoon. Mandy had explained the situation to her over the phone. She went to the garden gate to greet them. 'Hi, Elise. Thanks for coming.'

'Hi, Mandy. Hi, Mr and Mrs Hope,' said Elise, her face lighting up in a smile. 'It's no problem. We're only too glad to help. I can imagine what Julia must be going through.'

'Yes. It's a difficult situation,' said Emily Hope. 'Let's hope Mandy's idea works.'

As soon as Maisy caught sight of Mandy, her tail wagged back and forth in greeting. Mandy patted her. 'Hello, beautiful.'

The Dalmatian looked gorgeous with her bright eyes and prancing steps. The liver-brown spots seemed to stand out on her glossy coat. Mandy had never seen her looking happier.

'The Hamptons should be here soon,' Mandy told Elise. 'James is coming too. But he had to cycle over to Walton to collect something first.'

In fact, James had been very mysterious about where he was going. Mandy wondered what he was up to.

Elise touched Maisy's head to get her attention. Then she pointed to the ground. Maisy sat down at once, still looking up at her owner's face. Elise unclipped her dog's lead and after a waiting for a moment, held up her hand and opened and closed her fingers in a snapping movement. Maisy leaped forward at once and began racing around the garden.

That must be the sign for 'off you go', Mandy thought. She watched, fascinated, as Elise threw her dog a ball. Maisy stretched up to catch it, then came running back to her owner with the ball in her mouth. Her tail wagged nineteen to the dozen.

Mandy joined in the game. She tossed the ball in the air and Maisy caught it easily. Mandy threw it again and it fell short. But Maisy didn't care. She dashed at the ball, pushed it along the grass with her nose, then batted it with her big paws. Mandy, Elise and Mr and Mrs Hope laughed.

'Maisy looks so happy, doesn't she?' Mandy said to her mum and dad.

'She certainly does,' said Mrs Hope. 'How's she getting on with her silent whistle?'

'Just great,' said Elise. 'I'm so grateful to you for telling me about it. Let me show you.'

As she was taking the whistle out of her pocket, Julia and her parents came into the garden. Julia's father held Echo on a very short lead. The Dalmatian had her head down and her tail was tucked between her legs.

Mandy was struck by the difference in the two dogs – Maisy, so happy and boisterous, and poor Echo looking timid and unhappy.

'Hi,' Julia greeted Mandy. She looked really miserable. 'Dad has to hold Echo now. I can't control her on the lead at the moment.'

'Julia, Mr and Mrs Hampton, this is Elise,' Mandy said.

'Hello, Elise. Nice to meet you,' Mr and Mrs Hampton replied.

Julia said hello too. Then she seemed to spot

Maisy. 'Is that your dog?' she said to Elise in surprise.

They all looked down the garden to where Maisy was playing happily with her ball.

'Yes,' Elise said. 'That's Maisy. And this must be Echo. She looks like a lovely dog.'

'She is,' said Julia, sounding pleased.

'Is it safe for your dog to be running around like that?' Mr Hampton asked. 'I mean, won't she run off if she gets the chance?'

Elise shook her head. 'Oh, no. Maisy's responded really well to her training. I'll call her over so that you can say hello.'

Julia frowned, but she looked intrigued. 'How are you going to do that? She can't hear you, can she?'

'Not if I shout to her, no,' agreed Elise. 'But most deaf animals still have some degree of hearing. Emily told me about a special silent whistle that only dogs can hear.' She showed Maisy's whistle to Julia. 'You can buy them in most pet shops.' Elise blew the whistle, while Julia and her parents watched closely.

Maisy's head shot up and she looked round. With her ears pricked, she trotted straight over to Elise.

'Good girl.' Elise took her dog's face in her hands to praise her.

'That's amazing,' said Julia's dad.

'I'd never have believed it,' Mrs Hampton agreed.

Julia didn't say anything for a moment. She was staring down at Echo. 'Could you blow it again, please?' she said excitedly to Elise.

'Of course.' Elise gave two short blasts.

Echo's ears swivelled. She looked up at Julia, her eyes bright and her mouth open as though she was smiling. She'd heard the whistle!

'Mum! Dad! She heard it!' Tears glittered in Julia's eyes.

'That's brilliant!' Mandy said, glancing up at her mum with a lump in her throat.

Mrs Hope patted her arm. 'It looks like it's going well,' she whispered.

Just then James arrived looking rather red in the face. He dumped his bike on the grass and came over. 'Hi! What's happening?'

Mandy started to explain, then Julia took over. 'Echo heard the dog whistle! Isn't it wonderful?' she said excitedly.

'Wow!' said James. 'That's great. And it looks as if Echo and Maisy have made friends too.' The two Dalmatians were wagging their tails and sniffing each other. They made a handsome pair, Maisy with her liver and white colouring and Echo with her more traditional black and white spots.

'Why don't we let them play together?' suggested Elise. 'Echo will be quite safe. The garden is enclosed.'

Mr Hampton looked doubtful.

'Go on. Let her off the lead, Dad,' urged Julia. 'Poor Echo hasn't had a good run for days.'

Mr Hampton's face softened. He bent down to unclip the lead. 'I suppose it couldn't hurt.'

Maisy gave a joyful bark and darted away. Echo took off after her like a rocket. They dashed around play-biting and chasing each other.

'Echo looks just like her old self,' Julia said with delight. 'Look at her go!'

After watching the dogs play for a minute or two, James fished in his rucksack. He held out a coloured envelope to Mandy. 'Here you are. You tell me if these aren't prizewinners!'

'What?' Mandy opened the envelope and took out a pile of photographs. 'Oh, of course. I'd almost forgotten about these,' she said, beginning to leaf through them. Then her eyes opened wide as she looked at the photos of herself with Honey-

Mum and Sprite. 'These are really lovely,' she said.

The doe and fawn stood in the dappled sunlight beneath the trees. Their coats looked glossy and healthy. In one of the photos, Sprite's graceful neck was reaching forward so that she could nuzzle Mandy's hand.

Mr and Mrs Hope admired the photographs. 'I think you stand a good chance of winning a prize with those,' Adam Hope commented.

'This one is definitely my favourite!' Mandy declared, holding up the one of herself stroking Sprite.

James grinned. 'I wanted to surprise you, so I got them developed by the one-hour service in Walton.'

Mandy laughed. 'So that was the great mystery! These are brilliant photos. But you know what? I reckon you have some pretty good subjects here. You should take some of Maisy and Echo playing together!'

'Yeah!' James agreed. 'Maybe we can arrange it sometime.'

Mandy gave him a hopeful look. 'Fingers crossed,' she whispered.

They looked down the garden at the Dalmatians. Maisy was crouching down on her front paws. Echo stood over her, tail wagging. She barked and pretended to nip Maisy's tail. Then the two of them took off again.

'Echo seems a lot less nervous, doesn't she?' said Julia.

'Yes,' Mandy answered. 'Maybe she's starting to get her confidence back.'

'Do you think so?' asked Julia.

'Mandy's right,' Mrs Hope said. 'And it will help Echo if you start to feel more relaxed too, then she won't feel so jumpy.'

Julia blinked at her. 'Do you mean that because we've all been so tense and worried, some of that has rubbed off on to Echo?'

'Yes,' Mrs Hope confirmed gently. 'That's the way it works with pets. But it works the other way too.'

So far, so good, Mandy thought. She had an idea, and turned to Elise. 'Can you blow the whistle to call Maisy to you again, please?'

'Sure,' said Elise. She blew the whistle.

Maisy's ears pricked and she looked around. She gave a short bark and ran towards Elise.

Mandy watched Echo closely. The Dalmatian stood there, her ears twitching. She looked at Elise who was making a big fuss of Maisy. Then she looked at Julia. She whined softly, but stood her ground.

'That's it, girl!' said Julia. She turned to Mandy. 'Echo can definitely hear the whistle. But she doesn't realise she's supposed to come over.'

'Can we try that again, Elise?' Mandy asked.

Elise signed to Maisy to run down the garden again. Maisy and Echo began playing together. Elise let them become absorbed in their game for a few moments, then this time, she asked Julia to come and stand next to her. 'Ready?'

Julia bit her lip. 'OK.'

Elise blew the whistle. Once again Maisy ran straight back up the garden to her owner. Echo's ears pricked. She gave a short bark and dashed after Maisy. Then she came right up to Julia, her tail wagging eagerly.

'Give her lots of love and praise now, Julia!' said Elise.

Julia didn't need telling twice. She crouched down and cupped Echo's face as she had seen Elise and Mandy do. 'Clever, girl. Oh, you clever girl!' Julia's voice was choked with emotion as she rubbed her cheek against Echo's face. 'Mum! Dad! Did you see that? Wasn't she brilliant?'

Mrs Hampton looked delighted. She went over

to Echo. Then she too crouched down and put her hands gently around Echo's face. 'Good girl!' she said. Echo wagged her tail and gave a proud little bark.

Mr Hampton went over to praise Echo with the same actions. 'She seems so alert now. I would never have believed it,' he declared. 'This is amazing!'

Elise beamed at Julia. 'Echo picked that up really quickly. She's obviously very intelligent. Do you want to try a couple of hand signals, Julia?'

Julia nodded eagerly.

'OK. If she runs to you, you do this to stop her jumping up.' Elise bent slightly and held her arms out in front with her palms raised as if to say 'stop'.

Julia copied her. 'That's easy,' she said.

'This is the signal for "sit".' Elise held her fingers together and pointed to the ground. 'Use a sort of jabbing movement.'

Julia practised. 'Like this?' She pointed her fingers at the floor.

Elise nodded. 'That's it. Well done.'

Julia looked pleased. 'I think I'm getting the hang of it. It's not as difficult as I thought.'

'It's natural to be nervous. I was at first,' Elise admitted. 'But look at us now! With patience and lots of practice, Echo will soon be as confident as Maisy.'

'Could we come for walks with you and Maisy sometimes?' Julia asked hesitantly.

Elise gave her a warm smile. 'Of course you can. We'd love that.'

'And they could use our garden for Echo's training, so Julia needn't worry about Echo getting out, couldn't they?' Mandy said to her mum.

Mrs Hope smiled. 'Any time!'

Julia beamed. She already seemed more confident – just like Echo.

'And James and me will help with Echo's training too, won't we?' Mandy spoke up again. James nodded.

Julia turned eagerly to her parents. 'Do you hear that? Everybody wants to help! Oh, we can keep Echo now, can't we?'

Mr and Mrs Hampton were smiling broadly. They glanced at each other, then looked at Adam and Emily Hope. 'With Elise giving us a bit of training advice, I think we could manage,' Julia's dad said at last.

'Yeah!' Julia jumped up and down. 'That's fantastic!'

Julia's mum stroked Echo. 'I think Echo

deserves another chance. I hope she'll give us one too.'

'I thought you might be able to use this,' said Elise. She gave Julia a dog whistle. 'It's a spare one. You can use it until you get one for Echo.'

'Oh, thanks!' Julia looked delighted. She bent down and showed it to Echo. 'Look, this is for you!' Echo nudged the whistle with her black nose. Then she looked up at Julia and barked eagerly.

'I think she wants to try it out now!' laughed Julia.

Mandy thought she might burst with happiness. She grinned at her mum and dad, thrilled that her plan had worked. Echo and Julia were going to have so many good times together, and Mandy was sure it wouldn't be long before they were out enjoying long walks together in the dales again.